D1738473

BY ROBERT EMMET SHERWOOD

WATERLOO BRIDGE
THE QUEEN'S HUSBAND
THE ROAD TO ROME

CHARLES SCRIBNER'S SONS

WATERLOO BRIDGE

WATERLOO BRIDGE

A PLAY IN TWO ACTS

BY

ROBERT EMMET SHERWOOD

CHARLES SCRIBNER'S SONS

NEW YORK · LONDON

1930

WATERLOO BRIDGE

A PLAY IN TWO ACTS

BY

ROBERT EMMET SHERWOOD

"When the War is over and the Kaiser's out of print,
I'm going to buy some tortoises and watch the beggars sprint . . .
When the War is over and we've done the Belgians proud,
I'm going to keep a chrysalis and read to it aloud."
—A. A. MILNE.

CHARLES SCRIBNER'S SONS
NEW YORK · LONDON
1930

TO
MY WIFE

PREFACE

Two years before the war I looked at London through the eyes of the usual American tourist. I saw it as an enormous, opulent, pompous substance, full of confident superiority, red coats and red beef, dowdiness that transcended fashion, power in effect and incalculably more power in reserve, an imperturbable consciousness of Britain's vaunted "dominion over palm and pine," a tradition that was more stalwart and less perishable than any reality. There were blemishes, to be sure, on its vast, placid, smug countenance, but even these, because they were seen through the mellowed glass of Dickens, appeared to be charmingly "quaint" and "picturesque."

One of the weekly magazines published a group of paintings showing how London would look as a ruined city, crumbled and overgrown and deserted. These fanciful imaginings occasioned much satisfied laughter among the weekly's readers. The notion that London could ever decay was funny enough to be in *Punch*. London had been there, on the banks of the Thames, before the arrival of the Romans. It had continued to be there after the Romans went home. It had survived the invasions and wars of the Saxons, the Danes, the Normans and the Puritans. It had curled its lip at Napoleon Bonaparte, who had seen almost everything that there is to see on earth but who had not been permitted to look upon London.

It was freely admitted that St. Petersburg was founded on dynamite; that Berlin was a windbag, subject to deflation; that Paris had been on the decline ever since Sedan; that New York was merely a precocious colony, another Carthage, which could never hope to assume the dignity or importance enjoyed by its parent.

London was eternal. It would know occasional hard times, of course, due to the muddling policies of some liberal ministry, or to the bursting of some distant financial bubble. It would know wars through the columns of its press: Kipling wars, involving millions of black men and a brigade or so of indomitable but essentially humorous British Tommies.

Such minor disturbances would not bother London. It would go on—"business as usual"—adding to its wealth and its girth, drinking its honest, unemotional beer and eating its tasteless Sunday joint, erecting unsightly monuments to the great men that it was capable of producing.

The poor, said London, may always be with us—but so will the rich, the noble, the talented and the brave.

. . . This was in the summer of 1912.

Five years later, in November, 1917, I came back to the great, proud city as a private soldier on leave. I arrived at Waterloo Station (all Canadian soldiers always seemed to arrive at Waterloo, no matter where they might be coming from). I walked across Waterloo Bridge to the Strand, which was then a dark, sluggish river of khaki. Officers and men, from all those extensive areas that are colored pink on the map of the world, moved up and down the Strand, looking for something that wasn't there. On leave from France, Mesopotamia, the Channel patrol or the mine fields of the North Sea, thirsting for intoxicating hilarity, they resembled crowds of determined pleasure-seekers in an amusement park that has been closed for the winter.

London was not in ruins. The artist's fantastic prophecy had not actually been fulfilled. The Royal Standard still floated haughtily over Buckingham Palace; St. Paul's and the British Museum still stood firm; the Albert Memorial was still regrettably intact. Here and there, to be sure, were visible evidences of the destruction by enemy bombs—blasted buildings, craters in the embankment—but these were not important.

Nevertheless, something tremendous had gone out of London, and that something was the insular complacency, the all-conquering pride, which had made Britain universally great and, at the same time, universally unpopular. This pride had been killed in action in the war, and of all the dreadful losses that Britain sustained, this was the bitterest and the one that can never be replaced.

The late fall of 1917 saw the ebb-tide in the spirits of the tired, battered people of London. For more than three years they had been striving day and night to convince the world, and themselves, that all the Kaisers in creation couldn't affect London's ability to "carry on"; but the burden of this pretense was too much for human beings, even for English human beings, to bear. For there was no possible way of disguising the unlovely truth that this war had not been a success. It had required the expenditure of upward of three-quarters of a million British lives. It had absorbed everything in the way of money, industrial genius and fortitude that Britain could summon. It had accomplished nothing, as yet, and its end was immeasurably far away. As the British Empire had redoubled its efforts and its sacrifices, as it had yielded up enough of its flower and its nourishment to win a hundred of the wars it had known in the past, the chimera of victory grew less and less distinct until it vanished entirely. Men and women still said, as a matter of course, that this or that would "win the war"; but it was difficult to find any one who believed, in his heart, that the war would ever be won; the utmost that could be hoped for it was that some day, somehow, it would be finished.

In the previous spring there had been a momentary revival of the old 1914 enthusiasm. The United States came in, the Italians gained some mountain peaks, Kerensky promised to put new vigor into the liberated Russian horde, the Germans evacuated a large section of Picardy and the Canadians effected a spectacular advance at Vimy Ridge. But then the color of the prospect had changed. The United States, after its preliminary flourishes, contributed nothing but statements; most of the Americans who appeared in the war zone were not soldiers but congressmen on journeys of inspection. The counter-revolution in Russia brought technical peace to the eastern front, and Hindenburg was rushing his divisions westward. The Italian army collapsed miserably and was now regarded as a defunct factor in the Allied forces. There were ugly rumors, emphatically denied but alarmingly persistent, of a disastrous mutiny in the French army.

To counteract the baneful effect on civilian morale of all these discouragements, the British authorities deemed it wise to produce a few victories. They sent the over-worked Canadians and other storm troops against Passchendaele Ridge, which was a deep mound of mud on the nose of the Ypres salient and of no conceivable value to any one. It was ultimately taken, but whatever joy its capture may have brought to the voters at home was chilled by the staggering casualty lists that followed it. The Canadians saw many bad engagements in the war, from the first gas attack at Ypres in 1915 to the penetration of the almost impenetrable Drocourt-Quéant switch-line in September, 1918; but those who went through all the worst of them remember the assault on Passchendaele Ridge as the most terrible carnage of all.

Another attempt at sensational but fruitless victory was the sudden capture of Cambrai, the news

of which set the bells of London ringing and filled
the cathedrals with congregations of thanks givers,
and which was followed almost immediately by news
of the ferocious German counter-attack. When it
was learned that "some one had blundered," and
that thousands of Tommies had been killed or taken
prisoner, the devout expressions of gratitude were
turned into curses and protests against the incom-
petence and profligacy of the British high command.
(There is, by the way, a superb description of the
counter-attack at Cambrai by a Prussian officer,
Ernst Jünger, in his book "The Storm of Steel.")

It is easy to condemn these apparently wanton
sacrifices made at the command of the politicians
and the generals; but be it said for the politicians
and the generals that such actions seemed neces-
sary at the time. The situation was genuinely desperate and Great Britain, of all the original Allies,
was forced to meet it alone. The public spirit had
to be kept up, in France as well as in England, and
the only way that this could be accomplished was by
proof of ground actually gained, even if the ground
was admitted to be worthless. The ordinary tricks
of war-time propaganda, so freely and so effectually
used at that time in the United States, had been
worked to death in Europe. Years before the recruiting officers had been able to assure their audiences
that one Anglo-Saxon could whip ten Huns. But
the facts of the war had proved that this was not
true, and every day these facts came more disagree-
ably close to home. For the first time in almost a

thousand years England's sacred soil was being hit directly by the blows of an alien enemy.

The submarine blockade had been increased to such an extent that there was a real and imminent menace of starvation. It was almost impossible for the ordinary householder to obtain meat, except rancid bacon; sugar, butter, flour and eggs were priceless luxuries. Substitutes were available, but they were not convincing. There was a miserably insufficient supply of coal, and the possessor of a box of matches was looked upon with awe and envy.

Every clear, moonlit night London was subjected to attacks by the Gotha bombers. It is usual to think of these air-raids solely in terms of Zeppelins, which looked more menacing and were therefore suitable for spectacular effects in the movies; but the Gothas were far more effective and more to be feared. Adequate defenses had been devised against the cumbersome dirigibles. The swift, easily manoeuverable airplanes, however, could not be stopped. They came in relays, droned over London, dropped their bombs, and went home to prepare for another visit. Hundreds of batteries of anti-aircraft guns were placed about the city, creating an intense barrage that was more damaging than the planes themselves; it is probable that more people were killed by flying shrapnel than by bombs.

London, none too bright at best, was utterly dark at night. The globes of all street lamps were smeared with black paint. Automobile head-lights went out at the first suggestion of a warning. Any one who showed a light in a window was in danger of a visit from the police.

In the air-raid shelters—Underground stations and cellars—were strange gatherings of noblemen and navvies, most of them either very old or very young, some in evening dress, some in their night clothes, some playing bridge, some reading, some carrying on their domestic squabbles in strident tones. All of them were trying, in an obviously self-conscious manner, to appear unconcerned; and each of them, while recognizing that his neighbor's stoicism was no more genuine than his own, was infinitely comforted to know that whatever the circumstances Englishmen would not precipitate embarrassing scenes.

It was an incomparable performance of what Alexander Woollcott has correctly called "the tragedy of the stiff upper lip."

London was wearing its traditional armor of phlegm. Viewed from this remote distance (twelve years), that armor appears absurdly thin and false. One may truthfully say, "poor things—they were kidding themselves." But in 1917 the British phlegm was both an imperishable wall of defense and a saving grace. It caused the alien observer to realize that these people had not achieved their previous estate of world domination by accident. What they had gained they had earned.

I remember an article in *Punch* at that time, burlesquing the patriotic poetry which amateurs were then contributing to the correspondence col-

umns of the daily press. One of the examples of the
"right spirit" was as follows:

> "Though overhead the Gothas buzz,
> Stands London where it did? It does!"

Also in *Punch* was a picture of a pathetic little
man, a hawker, trying to sell kites to children on
Guy Fawkes day. Each kite was emblazoned with
the Union Jack. The hawker was shouting:

"'Ere you are. All the official 'oliday fun! Fly
the patriotic kites and annoy the Gothas!"

Another of *Punch's* gallant contributions to the
gaiety of a profoundly sad nation was a drawing by
the great George Belcher—a drawing, needless to
say, of two elderly Cockney women chatting over
their beer. They were discussing methods of deal-
ing with the air-raid problem.

"Well," said one of them, "I always runs about,
meself. You see, as my 'usband sez, an' very reason-
able, too, a movin' targit is more difficult to 'it."

The London theatres were packed. "Chu Chin
Chow" was in the third, or maybe the eleventh,
year of its run at His Majesty's. Mr. Gerald Du
Maurier was delighting the remnants of the carriage
trade in the new Barrie play, "Dear Brutus." C. B.
Cochrane was presenting Arthur Bourchier as Old
Bill in Captain Bruce Bairnsfather's unforgettable
"The Better 'Ole." In the leading cinema palaces
wounded Tommies and their girls were shuddering
together as they viewed the lurid scenes of Baby-
lonian bloodshed in D. W. Griffith's massive spec-
tacle, "Intolerance."

At the Hippodrome (I think it was the Hippodrome) little Daphne Pollard was appearing, dressed, approximately, as a doughboy, and giving a spirited rendition of a Yankee war-song which contained these encouraging lines:

"So prepare,
Say a prayer,
Send the word—send the word to beware . . ."

It went very well, especially when a huge canvas ocean liner lumbered in behind Miss Pollard and disgorged swarms of chorus girls who were also costumed, approximately, as "Sammies." They saluted smartly on the beat and snapped their hips in the Tiller manner.

Nevertheless, despite the cheery assurances from the reliable George M. Cohan, the belief existed among many who applauded his rousing song that it might well be over over here before the Yanks had arrived. There was a growing suspicion that President Wilson's dramatic declaration of war was the pardon that came too late. Eight months had elapsed since the welcome news sped out of Washington, and the U. S. army in the front line consisted (so far as any one knew) of one company of engineers.

New troops were being poured into France by the tens of thousands, but they were not Americans. They were Germans, transferred from the Masurian Lakes region and the now quiet Italian front. Their shadows were lengthening over Flanders, and the coal fields of Lens, and Picardy and Champagne,

and the shattered fortresses of Verdun. There was
in the air the swelling threat of a final, overwhelm-
ing offensive—a threat that came to realization on
the grey morning of March 21st, 1918, the occasion
of the last scene of "Journey's End."

England survived that ordeal, but came out of
it chastened, humbled, subdued, and ready to vote
into power the very men who had been all but hanged
for treason because they protested against the war
in 1914.   *   *   *

I returned to London a year later, in happier
times. The great offensive had rolled over most of
the old Western front, and there had been some
bad moments when it seemed that the British army
must abandon the channel ports and retreat to the
line of the river Somme to form, with the French,
a ring around Paris, leaving the defense of England
itself to the navy.* But this had not happened. The
Germans had been stopped, as much by the in-
fluenza epidemic as by allied strength.

Then, with astounding suddenness, a huge and
eager American Expeditionary Force was delivered in France, and July 14th saw the second
successful counter-attack from the Marne. On August 8th the British moved forward, the Hindenburg line was broken, and Wilson fired his fourteen
points into the crumbling structure of Mittel Europa.

In October, 1918, I was transferred to a hospital

---

* I don't know whether this plan of retreat was ever seriously
considered. All of my knowledge of the strategic conduct of the
war is based on latrine gossip.

in Bushy Park, not far from Hampton Court, in the environs of London. We were mostly "walking cases" in that hospital—that is to say, patients whose cures had largely been effected elsewhere and who were now undergoing special conditioning treatment. We were allowed to go out in the afternoons and early evenings; but we wore the regulation hospital blue uniforms (much like the modern beach pajamas) which identified us as convalescents. It was against the law to serve liquor to any wearer of this uniform, but there were various means of evading that prohibition.

London no longer gave the effect that it was perilously close to the deep end. There were far more men on leave, due to the extent of front line that had been taken over by the Americans. The submarine blockade had been petering out, and a strict but sensible rationing system had worked to provide an equable distribution of food. The hunter's moon waxed and waned and brought with it no Gotha bombers.

Every one knew that peace was near at hand. It might possibly come before Christmas, or it might be delayed for another year; but it was unmistakably on the way, and the weary, fed up people were trying to imagine what it would be like. They could no more envisage the circumstances of existence after the war than they could envisage the life after death. It was a hazy, incredible blur, but it was infinitely pleasant to contemplate.

In the morning of November 11th we were lined up in the stable yard at the hospital (it was a converted country house) waiting for our mail, which was delivered from an office that had once been a box stall. All of us had been wondering whether the command to cease firing would be issued before we were given clean bills of health and sent back to the line.

An Army Medical Corps sergeant appeared in the yard, blew his whistle, and instructed us to report to the Y. M. C. A. hut.

We went there, listlessly, and when we had assembled, the elderly chaplain (who had been invalided from France because he had organic heart disease) stepped up on the platform and asked us to join him in a prayer of thanks to God, because the war was over.

So we said the prayer, and sang "God Save the King," and cheered Field-Marshal Haig and General Currie. Then some of us sneaked out through the barbed-wire fence about the hospital grounds, and climbed on a Hammersmith 'bus, and rode into the insane bewilderment of London's celebration, in which I for one remained for a week, absent without leave.

On the way in our 'bus passed a ploughed field (every square inch of ground was cultivated) where some German prisoners were at work. We shouted at them, "Hey, Heinie—the war's over!" But they only grinned and waved at us amicably—not understanding, or not caring.

For several days the Strand and Trafalgar Square and all surrounding thoroughfares were jammed with the wildest mob that I have ever seen or, I hope, will ever see. There had been rows of captured cannon along the Mall, and these had been seized by wild Australians and Canadians, who were always the riffraff of the British army, and formed into a bonfire at the base of the Nelson monument. This fire was kept going for hours—perhaps for days; I don't clearly remember. The flames enveloped the column of the monument and seriously threatened to cremate Lord Nelson himself. The London fire department fought manfully to check this destructive enthusiasm, but the hilarious Colonials captured the hose and turned it on the firemen.

Throughout the turmoil, the King and Queen and Princess Mary drove through the crowds, in an open carriage with no attendants, smiling and bowing and acknowledging salutes. Their Majesties seemed to be particularly delighted to see soldiers climbing up the lamp-posts to scrape the black paint off the globes, exactly in the manner of snake-dancers clambering up the goal-posts after the big game.

London's protracted orgy was not a celebration of victory. None of the rioters suggested hanging the Kaiser in effigy, or shouting "We beat the Bosches" or "What price 'Indenburg now?" All that any one was thinking—and it was almost more than any one could conceive—was that the bloody business was over with.

While I was watching the fire in Trafalgar Square

I found myself jammed in the mob next to a very short and quite pretty girl in a blue tailored suit. Across her shirtwaist she had pinned a silk American flag.

I asked her why she was wearing that.

"Because it belongs to me, you big Limey," she answered, in a tone that suggested nothing but Broadway.

Then I asked her how she happened to be in this town, of all places, and she told me that she had come over years before in the chorus of "The Pink Lady," and had stuck, through no choice of her own. She also told me that she had a nice little flat near Leicester Square, and why not come up some time soon?

Unfortunately, I forgot the address in the heat of the moment, so I never saw her again. But I have written about her and about London in this play, which is sentimental, but justifiably so.

R. E. S.

"WATERLOO BRIDGE"

Presented by Charles Dillingham at the Tremont Theatre, Boston, Mass., November 21st, 1929, at the Broad Street Theatre, Philadelphia, Pa., December 23rd, and at the Fulton Theatre, New York City, January 6th, 1930, with the following cast:

KITTY	Cora Witherspoon
MILITARY POLICEMAN	Hannam Clark
GERTRUDE	Eunice Hunt
OFFICER	George G. Wallen
SERGEANT-MAJOR	Alexander Frank
SERGEANT	Douglas Garden
MYRA	June Walker
SAILOR	William Evans
CIVILIAN	Herbert Saunders
AUSTRALIAN	Allan Fagan
ROY CRONIN	Glenn Hunter
MRS. HOBLEY	Florence Edney

Staged by Winchell Smith

WATERLOO BRIDGE

CAST

(In the order of first appearance)

KITTY
A MILITARY POLICEMAN
GERTRUDE
AN OFFICER
A SERGEANT-MAJOR
A SERGEANT
MYRA
A SAILOR
A CIVILIAN
AN AUSTRALIAN
ROY CRONIN
A CONSTABLE
MRS. HOBLEY
A LABORER
HIS WIFE

SCENES

ACT I:

SCENE   I.   *Waterloo Bridge, London.*
            Eleven o'clock in the evening of a November day in 1917.

SCENE II.   *Myra's room in Mrs. Hobley's lodging house.*
            A few minutes later.

ACT II:

SCENE   I.   *Myra's room.*
            Noon, the next day.

SCENE II.   *Waterloo Bridge.*
            The same evening.

ACT I
SCENE I

WATERLOO BRIDGE

ACT I

SCENE I

A bay in the wall on the eastern side of Waterloo Bridge.

The wall is well down stage, so that there is barely room in the foreground for what would be the sidewalk of the bridge.

In the recess of the wall is a long bench. At the extreme right and left are high lamps, the globes of which have been smeared with black paint so that they give only a murky light. There is very strong moonlight.

There is nothing beyond the wall, except perhaps the sombre suggestions of buildings and the dome of St. Paul's to the eastward. There are no lights whatever in the buildings.

Now and then, throughout this scene, there should be heard the whistles of river boats.

KITTY *is seated on the bench, eating an apple. She is a blatant London tart, profoundly pessimistic but meticulously cheerful, about thirty-five,*

7

*heavily painted, and conveying only occasional
suggestions of the charm she might once have pos-
sessed.*

*She is looking casually to right and to left,
along the bridge, as she eats—watching for cus-
tomers. When she sees a soldier coming she tosses
the core of the apple over the wall, swallows
hastily, pulls up her skirt a bit, and assumes an
alluring pose.*

A MILITARY POLICEMAN *comes in from the
right. He wears the regulation Tommy's uniform.
On his sleeve is a red band with the initials
"M. P." in blue letters. He carries a stout cane.*

MILITARY POLICEMAN

Evening, Kitty.

KITTY

Oh—it's you, is it? Good evening.

MILITARY POLICEMAN

What are you doing?

KITTY

I've been 'aving my supper. But I threw it into
the river when I saw you coming.

MILITARY POLICEMAN

You needn't 'ave minded me. I couldn't 'ave
accepted your kind invitation to join you. I'm
on duty.

KITTY

That's my complaint against you M. P.'s.
You're always on duty.

MILITARY POLICEMAN

Oh, well—some one 'as to keep the peace.

KITTY

Peace! (*She laughs.*) You *are* a wit.

MILITARY POLICEMAN (*looking toward the river*)
Lovely evening, ain't it?

KITTY

It's a 'orrible evening.

MILITARY POLICEMAN

Lovely for Fritzie, I mean. 'Ow's trade?

KITTY

Never been worse. What's 'appened to the
army?

MILITARY POLICEMAN

They've suffered a lot of casualties, that's
what's 'appened. They ain't being too free with
their leaves.

KITTY

It's bloody mismanagement, if you should ask
me. I give you my word—not ten men 'as crossed
this bridge in the past hour.

MILITARY POLICEMAN

It's the moon, sweet'eart—the beautiful full moon—the fox-'unters' delight.

KITTY

The fox-'unters can 'ave it—and the bombs that come with it. I wish the blasted thing'd go into a clipse and stay there.

MILITARY POLICEMAN

Why not try writing to *The Times* about it? (GERTRUDE *comes in from the right.*)

KITTY

'Ullo, Gertrude. 'Ow's luck?

GERTRUDE (*crossing*)

Ain't none. (*To* MILITARY POLICEMAN.) 'Ullo, red-band.

MILITARY POLICEMAN

Good evening to *you*.

KITTY

Where *you* going?

GERTRUDE

To Waterloo Station to meet the South'ampton train.

KITTY

Expecting any one?

GERTRUDE (*going on*)

No—just 'oping. . . . Toodleoo, Kitty.

KITTY

'Bye, Gertrude.

(GERTRUDE *goes out at the left.*)

MILITARY POLICEMAN

All the best. . . . You ought to go with 'er. That South'ampton train is apt to be loaded with sailors.

KITTY

Don't I know it? I got one of them once. 'E 'adn't a penny but he grew so fond of me 'e deserted. I thought I was going to 'ave 'im on my 'ands for the duration.

MILITARY POLICEMAN

Look sharp, there! (*An* OFFICER *comes in from the right. The* M. P. *stiffens to attention and salutes. The* OFFICER *returns the salute in an off-hand manner and goes out.*) My word—that gave me a start! I must be off. If I was caught loitering with you, they'd strip me of my arm-band and send me back to the war.

KITTY

We mustn't let that 'appen. I couldn't bear to lose you. I 'ave few enough friends among the police.

MILITARY POLICEMAN (*looking toward the left*)

'Ere comes some trade for you now. I'll go this way so as not to frighten 'em.

KITTY

You *are* kind.

MILITARY POLICEMAN

Well—cheero, Kitty.

KITTY

Night, night.

(*He goes out at the right. A* SERGEANT-MAJOR *and a* SERGEANT *come in from the left. They are very smart and impressive. They barely glance at* KITTY *as they pass.*)

SERGEANT-MAJOR

. . . I tried to show him 'ow wrong he was, and at the same time flatter 'im into thinking I was agreeing with him. But you know 'ow these Sandhurst lads put it on . . .

SERGEANT

Don't I!

KITTY

Evening, sergeants.

(*They pause and glare at her.*) *Page 13*

SERGEANT-MAJOR

Eh? What's that?

KITTY

I merely said "Good evening."

SERGEANT

A bloody tart.

KITTY

Oh, yes? Well, I wasn't even speaking to you.

SERGEANT

Who were you speakin' to, then?

KITTY

To the Sergeant-Major.

SERGEANT-MAJOR

Thank you—but the Sergeant-Major isn't taking any of you—not to-night.

SERGEANT

It's shameful 'ow this bridge is being infested with prostitutes. One can't move a step without being solicited. (*They move on.*)

KITTY (*going after them*)

That's the curse of this war, ain't it—prostitutes and sergeants?

SERGEANT-MAJOR

Be careful who you speak to—or you'll be reported to the military police.

KITTY

Oh, don't mind me, Sergeant-Major. I'm just a 'appy-go-lucky type. I always 'ave a cheery word for the troops—Britannia's pride! Boys of the bull-dog breed! (*She follows this with an obscene noise.*)

SERGEANT

'Arken to 'er.

KITTY

Now run along, mates. I'm expectin' my fiancy
'ere any minute and 'e might not understand my
familiarity with you.

SERGEANT (*incredulous*)

Your *fiancy?*

KITTY

Yes—'e's a general, 'e is, and 'e 'as a peculiar
dislike for sergeants.

SERGEANT

Do you 'ear that, Sergeant-Major? A blinkin'
general, no less. (*He laughs heartily.*) Perhaps
if you wait 'ere long enough, in all this moonlight, old 'Indenburgh himself will be over in one
of his bleeding Zeppelins to kiss you with a bomb.

SERGEANT-MAJOR

That's enough, Sergeant. Leave 'er alone.

KITTY

And you aren't going to ask me to 'ave a bite
to eat with you?

SERGEANT-MAJOR

No, thank you. We're both married men. Come
on.

KITTY (*as they go out at the right*)

Oh—you're both married, eh! To each other?

(She sings after them, "If you want to find the Sergeants, I know where they are, I know where they are. . . .")

(MYRA comes in from the left. She is small and pert and pretty, but jaded and fed up. She is American, with a few Cockney mannerisms in her speech that have been acquired during her four years in England. She is dressed in a shabby tailored suit, and is carrying an ancient suitcase.)

MYRA

Hello, Kitty.

KITTY *(peering at her)*

Who's that?

MYRA

Don't you remember me?

KITTY

Why—if it ain't the Yank. 'Ul*lo*, Myra! *(They embrace.)* We'd about given you up. 'Ow've you been, ducky, and when did you get back?

MYRA

I just pulled in to Waterloo Station.

KITTY

I'd begun to think we was never going to see you again.

MYRA

Well—here I am!

KITTY

My—I *am* glad to 'ave you back, ducky! It's been months since I saw you.

MYRA

It seems like years. I'd forgotten what this town looks like.

KITTY

And 'ow did you enjoy the farming?

MYRA

Well—I found out that girls like you and me wasn't built for working on a farm.

KITTY

I could've told you that in the first place. Where'd you go?

MYRA

Oh, I was in Kent for a while . . .

KITTY

Tending the 'ops, I suppose.

MYRA

Sure—and then they shifted me to a God-forsaken little hole down in Surrey.

KITTY

What a 'orrible experience! But you're looking fit, I must say.

MYRA

Oh, it's a healthy life, for those that like health.

KITTY

'Ave you got any money?

MYRA

The last time I counted it was three shillings.

KITTY

Didn't they pay you for your farmerette duty?

MYRA

They did not. All I got was board. You see, I was doing patriotic service.

KITTY

Well, I've been doing patriotic service, too. All I get is the M. P.'s telling me to move on.

(GERTRUDE *comes in from the left, arm in arm with a* SAILOR, *who is walking very fast.*)

GERTRUDE

You're fair getting me out of breath.

SAILOR

You'll 'ave to kick it up a bit, my girl, if you're coming along wi' me.

(GERTRUDE *waves to* KITTY *as she follows the* SAILOR *out.*)

MYRA

Gertie, wasn't it?

KITTY

Yes—and look what's she's got! Whoops— ain't she naval!

Myra

I hate sailors.

Kitty

You're like me, ducky—always loyal to the army.

(Myra *has been looking across the bridge toward the ominous bulk of London.*)

Myra

How is business around this old graveyard?

Kitty

Shocking. This war . . .

Myra

I know. I've been reading the Sunday papers. We don't seem to be going so good these days.

Kitty

The bloody Russians 'ave given in. The Italians 'as gone 'ome in disgust—and as for us! Why, only last week they were 'olding thanksgiving services 'ere for the great victory we won at Cambrai. There were crowds in all the churches. And even while the bells of St. Paul's and the Abbey were ringing out in celebration, the boys in the streets were shouting news of the German counter-attack and 'ow we'd lost I don't know 'ow many thousand men. Oh, it's ap*pall*ing!

MYRA

I noticed the people in the station, and in the streets coming over. They looked as if they was all hurrying to a funeral or something.

KITTY

That's just what they are doing. I give you my word, London's dead. Nothing fit to eat or drink, no signs of life and no 'ope of any. It's going to be a wretched winter.

MYRA

It must be terrible for us.

KITTY

It's ruinous. What are your plans?

MYRA

I ain't made any. I don't suppose there's any shows going into rehearsal?

KITTY

None that I know of. Will you go back to Mrs. 'Obley's to live?

MYRA

I guess so. Is it still there?

KITTY

Oh, yes. It's just the same. The old girl's as preachy as ever.

MYRA

Well—I'm used to her.

KITTY

I'm afraid Mrs. 'Obley won't welcome you very cordially if you 'ave no money.

MYRA

She's got all my stuff there. She's been holding it for what I owe her.

KITTY

If you're counting on any kindness from 'er you'll go to bed 'ungry.

MYRA

I'll be lucky to go to bed at all. She'll holler for the room rent in advance. Say—you couldn't stake me to a few shillings for a couple of days, could you, Kitty?

KITTY

P. 22

If I only *could*. But Yank, if you've got three bob you're better off than me. . . . 'Ullo! What's this? Oh—it's only a civvie!

(*She has started toward the right, but has turned away in disappointment. . . . An elderly* CIVILIAN *comes in from the right. He is poorly dressed, but gentle in speech and courtly in manner. He approaches* KITTY *and lifts his hat.*)

CIVILIAN

I beg pardon, Miss ——

KITTY (*affably*)

Yes?

CIVILIAN

Am I right for Balham?

KITTY

*Bal*ham? You can take a 'lectric train at Waterloo that'll fetch you there.

CIVILIAN

I—I think I'd rather walk.

KITTY

It's a long way, sir. . . .

CIVILIAN

But it's such a fine night—clear, bracing air.

KITTY (*with a glance at* MYRA)

Well—you keep straight on Waterloo Road, and then bear off on Kennington Park Road. But it's miles and miles.

CIVILIAN

I'll be all the better for a walk. Thank you so much. (*He lifts his hat.*) Good evening. (*He starts out.*)

KITTY

Good evening to you, sir. (*The* CIVILIAN *is gone.*) Poor old codger. The trouble with 'im is 'e ain't got the price of a thripenny ticket. 'E'll be fagged out before 'e ever sees Balham.

MYRA

I can sympathize with him. I had to walk all the way over the Hog's-back to Guildford this afternoon, lugging this damned bag.

KITTY

And no one to give you a lift?

MYRA

God, no. You don't see many cars on the roads these days.

KITTY

I know. Most of the taxis 'ere 'as stopped running. Nobody can get any petrol except the blinking red tabs. I expect you're too tired to go to work to-night.

MYRA

You're damned right I am. All I want to do is go to bed—and when I get there, I want to go to sleep.

KITTY

You're a lazy one. What you ought to do is come with me along the Strand and make some money so you can surprise Mrs. 'Obley with the rent.

MYRA (*looking along the bridge*)

The way it looks to me there ain't any money on the streets to-night.

KITTY

Oh— it'll be better later—after the raid's over.

MYRA

Is there going to be one?

KITTY

Course there is. That's why the bridge is so empty. Everyone's in the tubes and shelters already.

MYRA

We didn't get any of that stuff down in the country.

KITTY

Well, Fritzie never misses a clear night 'ere. And I can promise you its been raising 'ell with trade—keeps the soldiers off the streets. (*She looks upward.*) The dirty 'Un.

MYRA

Well, cheer up, Kitty. With the cold weather coming on, maybe it'll get foggy.

KITTY

That's all the protection we can expect. Fog! You never see our Flying Corps driving the 'Un back. If they were on the job, the Gothas and Zeppelins wouldn't get beyond Margate. (*An Australian soldier comes in from the left, whistling cheerily the march song, "Colonel Bogey."*) 'I, Australia—lookin' for a nice girl? (*He thumbs his nose and goes out.*) Bloody Colonial! Oh—Lord—trade is shocking bad. You can't persuade people to think about pleasure when they've got the wind up.

MYRA (*she has again been regarding the dismal prospect of London*)

Oh—it's a rotten town.

KITTY (*indignant*)

What is?

MYRA

London.

KITTY

I resent that!

MYRA

Well, what do you think of it, yourself?

KITTY

I 'ave a right to complain about it, cause I'm native. You ain't. You're a guest.

MYRA

Sure—just the same as a crook that's sent up is a guest in prison. And that's what London means to me. When I walked out of that station and felt the old pavements under my feet, I said to myself, "Oh, God! Do I have to start pounding *those* again!" I tell you, Kitty—farming is tough work, and it's dull—but it's a damned sight better than this.

KITTY (*knowingly*)

I see, ducky. Being out in the open air so much 'as made you virtuous.

MYRA

No, it ain't made me virtuous. It's made me homesick. It's made me wish I was out of this country of yours.

KITTY (*injured*)

That's gratitude, that is. After the way we've befriended you, and treated you as one of us, and . . .

MYRA

Oh, now, don't take it that way, Kitty. You can't blame me for thinking how swell it would be to be back in New York, where there's no war, and plenty of money, and electric lights . . .

KITTY

Yes—and if you were there, you'd be doing the same thing you're doing 'ere, wouldn't you?

MYRA

A fat chance! Why, if I was home, I might get another job in the chorus, and have the men running after *me*, instead of me running after them.

KITTY

The trouble with you is you're getting snobbish.

MYRA

Say—that's just what I'd like to get. I'd like to think I was the Queen of the Follies—and every time I'd walk out of the stage door in Forty-first street, the whole carriage trade'd be there, fighting to get at me. . . . The thing I hate is the walking up and down, up and down, all day, all night—chasing after bums, like that sailor Gertie was with. And having to listen to them telling you to get the hell out of the way, you bloody tart. . . . That's why I ain't in love with the idea of getting back to London.

KITTY

That's all very fine. But 'ere you are—back on the old bridge—and what are you going to *do* about it?

MYRA

I'm going back to work and get sore feet like I used to do.

KITTY (*sympathetic*)

I understand 'ow you feel, ducky. But it'll seem better after you've 'ad a good night's rest.

MYRA

Say—I think I'll change my mind about to-night.

KITTY

'Ow?

MYRA

I think I'll just go and drop this bag at Hobley's and then start out.

KITTY

You mean on the job?

MYRA

On the job. If I wait till to-morrow, it'll only be that much harder.

KITTY (*delighted*)

That's more like it, ducky! That's the stuff to give the troops. Now you're sounding like your old self again.

MYRA

It'll be great to see all the girls again. Agnes, and Phœbe, and Harriet, and . . .

KITTY

Phœbe's gone to Aldershot, but you'll find plenty of the others. Why not walk with me as far as the Strand?

MYRA

No—you go on ahead. You might meet a customer, and I'd be in the way, with this suitcase.

KITTY

You're very thoughtful. . . . I may see you a bit later on. . . .

MYRA

I hope so.

KITTY

And if we don't meet before morning, I'll come across the roof and call on you. Right?

MYRA

Sure. . . . Good luck, Kitty.

KITTY (*on the way out*)

No luck now, I'm afraid. There's too much of this bloody moonlight.

(*After* KITTY'*s exit,* MYRA *starts to pick up her suitcase—but looks to the left and sees* ROY *coming. As he enters, he pauses to gaze over the parapet at the impressive prospect of St. Paul's Cathedral by moonlight. . . .* ROY *is a palpable, forthright soldier, with a red, honest face. His ill-fitting but clean uniform is marked with the shining insignia of the Royal Canadian Regiment. On each sleeve is a Lance Corporal's chevron; on his left sleeve, a gold wound stripe. A haversack is slung over his shoulder. . . .* MYRA *takes a good look at him. . . . As he is passing her she makes an apparently awkward movement with her suitcase so that she shoves it in his path, and he stumbles over it.*)

MYRA

Oh—I'm *terribly* sorry . . .

Roy

Oh—that's all right . . .

Myra

It was very clumsy of me, but I . . .

Roy (*moving off*)

Never mind. No harm done.

Myra

I guess I didn't know which way I was going. (*She affects to be bewildered by the immensity of London.*)

Roy

You a stranger here?

Myra

Yes—I—I just arrived at the station, and I couldn't seem to pick up a taxi anywhere, and I'm kind of . . .

Roy

Say! You talk like an American.

Myra

That's what I am, soldier,

Roy

Well, I'll be darned. What are you doing here? I mean, how do you happen to be in this town?

MYRA

Oh—I've been over here doing war work.

ROY

Well! You and me both.

MYRA

Are you an American?

ROY

Why, sure! Couldn't you tell that just to listen to me?

MYRA

Well—I thought that was an English uniform.

ROY

Oh, don't let that fool you. It's Canadian. There's lots of us in this outfit.

MYRA

You were one of the boys that couldn't wait, weren't you? (*She is making no secret of her admiration.*)

ROY (*laughing sheepishly*)

Well—I guess so—but, say—I certainly am glad to hear the sound of your voice. It's been a long time since I've heard a woman talk like that. Where do you come from?

MYRA

I was last seen in New York.

ROY

New York City?

MYRA

Yes.

ROY

I come from up-State. Locke's Falls.

MYRA

Is that so?

ROY

Ever been there?

MYRA

No—I've never been to Locke's Falls.

ROY

Well, I guess you haven't missed much. But I like it. How long have you been here in London?

MYRA

Four years.

ROY

You mean to say you were here before the war? (*He can't imagine that any one was here before the war.*)

MYRA

Yes. I saw it start.

ROY

What were you—just on a trip?

MYRA

I came over with a show.

ROY

You mean, like a play?

MYRA

A musical show.

ROY

No! You're an actress?

MYRA

No—not exactly. I'm a chorus girl. (*She says this in the hope that it will impress and excite him. It does.*)

ROY

A chorus girl! Gosh . . .

MYRA

I guess that sounds pretty awful to you.

ROY

It does not. . . . It sounds fine to me! What —what was the name of the show you came over with?

MYRA

It was called "The Pink Lady."

ROY

Well—can you beat that! "The Pink Lady"! Why, I saw that in Syracuse. That was one good show, all right. Were you in it then?

MYRA

No—I missed Syracuse.

ROY

I suppose it was kind of a second-rate company that played it there. But it certainly was a great hit. I can remember every bit of it.

MYRA

Yes—everybody seemed to like it.

ROY

It certainly surprises me to meet anybody who was in "The Pink Lady." Are you still on the stage?

MYRA

No—I gave that up.

ROY

Got sick of it, I suppose?

MYRA

Yes, I got sick of it. And on top of that, I couldn't get a job.

ROY

Ah—I'll bet they don't know what talent is over here.

MYRA

Perhaps that's it.

Roy

So you've been doing war work. What kind?

Myra

Does it seem to you that you're asking a lot of questions?

Roy

I'm sorry, Miss. You probably think I'm pretty fresh. But, honestly—you don't know what your voice did to me. It just took me back home, and I guess you know what a long way that is.

Myra

Sure—that's all right. (*He gives evidence of starting to leave; she draws him back with a hasty question.*) Have you just come from the front?

Roy

Oh, no. I've been in hospital. I'm on sick leave.

Myra (*very solicitous*)

Were you wounded?

Roy

Yes—I got a nice little Blighty.

Myra

Oh—you poor thing! Whereabouts did it get you?

ROY

Shoulder and legs.

MYRA

All at once?

ROY

Well—it was just a machine gun. (*He indicates his right shoulder.*) And then I got some splinters before they'd scraped me up.

MYRA (*looking him over*)

But you're all well now, aren't you?

ROY

I ought to be. They've been working on me since last April.

MYRA

And you've been in hospital all that time!

ROY

Oh, well. There's lots worse places than hospital. . . .

MYRA

Well—I'm afraid I'll have to be moving along.

ROY

Where were you going?

MYRA

Oh—I have a little flat that I always go to when I'm in London. It's a tiny place—but it has a nice, homelike atmosphere.

Roy

Are you walking there?

Myra

I'm afraid I'll have to. There doesn't seem to be a sign of a taxi. . . . I suppose *you'll* be going out to see the town?

Roy

Say—the only thing I want to see now is some food. I'm so hungry I could . . . What's that?

Myra

Say! Listen! (*There is a dreadful shriek from a warning siren, followed by the sound of distant artillery.*) There it comes!

Roy

It sounds like the guns were opening up. . . . What's the idea?

(*The barrage increases. Mixed with it are the sounds of bugles, whistles and more sirens screaming the alarm.*)

Myra

Heinie's up.

(*Two civilians run across from right to left.*)

Roy (*excited*)

No! Is it an air raid?

MYRA

That's just what it is. We'd better be moving . . .

(*A shrill voice is heard shouting, "Take cover! Take cover!"*)

ROY

I've always wanted to see a raid on London. (*He is looking over the parapet toward the east. He takes out a cigarette.*)

MYRA

If you stay here you're liable to see too much of it.

ROY

Why—the chances are a million to one against a bomb dropping around here.

MYRA

It isn't the bombs that make it dangerous to be out. It's the shrapnel from our own guns. It comes down over the city like a rain-storm.

ROY

Just the same, it sure is something to see. . . . Just think of the old guy up there with eight million people to aim at. (*He starts to light his cigarette. She jumps forward and blows out the match.*) *Don't light that match Page 38*

MYRA

~~Don't be a damned fool!~~

ROY

What's the matter?

MYRA

You could go to jail for showing a light.

ROY

Gosh—this is funny. I thought I was on leave,
away from the war.

MYRA

You can't get away from this war, soldier. . . .
Well, I'm going.

ROY

Here—give me that grip. (*He takes her suitcase away from her.*) Where are you going?

MYRA

I don't know, but I'm not going to stay
here . . .

Read   (*A special constable, wearing a tin hat, rides
in on a bicycle, shouting, "Take cover! Take
cover!" and rides out.*) *Page 39 —*

ROY

There's a job I'd like to have.

MYRA

Are you coming? Or will you give me back my
suitcase?

Roy

Couldn't we go and get something to eat?

Myra

No—all the places close up during the raids. Come on!

Roy

All right—anywhere you say.

(*She goes out at the right. He follows her. The barrage has increased in volume as more batteries have opened up. The bugle calls, sirens and cries of "Take cover!" are heard from all directions. Bursts from machine guns are added to the general uproar. And there is one other sound: the vibrant, rhythmic hum of German airplane motors.*)

Curtain

(*The lowering of the curtain muffles the sound of the barrage, which continues to be heard, dimly, during the brief intermission between scenes and intermittently throughout most of the scene that follows.*)

ACT I
SCENE II

ACT I

SCENE II

A room in MRS. HOBLEY'S *lodging house in one of the mean streets between Aldwych and Covent Garden. The furniture is cheaply elegant but shabby. There is a table in the centre, a bed against the wall at the right, a door at the left, a window at the back, a washstand, bureau, dressing-table and several chairs. At the right is* MYRA'S *battered trunk, with a label, "The Pink Lady—Hotel." There is an antiquated gramophone on a small table near the bed at the right; it has a horn shaped and colored like a morning glory. On the walls are some pictures—one a shiny photographic portrait of* EDWARD VII *and the rest chromos of various sentimental scenes.*

MRS. HOBLEY *is at the window, which is somewhat to the right of centre. She is drawing the curtains so that no crack of light can emerge between the lowered shade and the sill.*

The gramophone is playing the "Beautiful Lady" waltz from "The Pink Lady." This should be heard before the curtain goes up.

MRS. HOBLEY *is a woman of about forty, with a few pathetic simulations of refinement. On her face is a permanent expression of resignation,*

43

P. 44

with which are mixed suspicion and scorn. She is in a constant stage of lamentation because she, a flagrantly good woman, has been compelled by force of wartime circumstance to subsist on the profits of the prostitution that goes on under her roof. At present, her one aim in life is self-justification.

MYRA *comes in.*

MYRA

Hello—Mrs. Hobley.

MRS. HOBLEY

What? Who's that? Oh! So you've come back, 'ave you?

MYRA

Weren't you expecting me?

MRS. HOBLEY

Yes—I 'ad your letter.

MYRA

Can I have the room?

MRS. HOBLEY

The room is to let, as you may see. *(She has turned off the gramophone, abruptly, without lifting the needle.)*

MYRA

That's fine.

MRS. HOBLEY

The first week will be payable strictly in advance.

MYRA

Well—you'll have to . . .

MRS. HOBLEY

So I'll trouble you for twenty-two shillings.

MYRA

What? Twenty-two shillings? Why you only used to charge me fourteen . . .

MRS. HOBLEY

Conditions that are painful to me 'ave forced me to raise the rent.

MYRA

But that's terrible. You've got no right to ask that much for a dump like this.

MRS. HOBLEY

While you've been away—wherever you 'ave been—you've probably managed to forget that there's such a thing as a war going on. Everything's dearer. It's all I can do to make body and soul meet. Twenty-two shillings for a sunny, airy apartment like this is little enough, and if you don't agree, you're invited to look elsewhere.

MYRA

Where's my trunk?

MRS. HOBLEY

I 'ave it in safe keeping.

MYRA

I notice you've been playing my gramophone and wearing out the records.

MRS. HOBLEY

That gramophone is not yours. It's mine, and so's your trunk mine, and all its contents, and they'll remain mine until such time as you pay me in full for what's been owing since last April. You'll see the itemized bill on the dresser there.

MYRA (*looking at the bill*)

Well—I'll take the room back, for the time being. But you'll have to wait a little while for the first payment.

MRS. HOBLEY

Oh, will I? I'm not so sure that I will. I notice you 'ave no luggage with you.

MYRA

Yes, I have. But it . . .

MRS. HOBLEY

I suppose you left it at the Carlton, eh?

MYRA

No—it's being brought up by—by a friend of mine . . .

MRS. HOBLEY

A gentleman friend?

MYRA

Yes—a gentleman.

MRS. HOBLEY (*pretending to be pained*)
Indeed! Up to your old ways, aren't you?

MYRA

It's none of your business what I'm doing.

MRS. HOBLEY

Don't be insolent with me, you common little miserable street walker. None of my business, eh!

MYRA

No—it isn't. I don't owe you anything. You've got my trunk and most of my clothes in your possession.

MRS. HOBLEY

And a valuable wardrobe it is. I couldn't even give it away to the Salvation Army. I want my pay, in money. That's the very least I 'ave a right to demand.

MYRA

You'll get your money, all right. *Page 48*

MRS. HOBLEY

When? After your gentleman 'as paid up for 'is licentious enjoyment?

MYRA

I told you you'd be paid. Now will you kindly get to hell out of here?

MRS. HOBLEY

Yes—curse at me. You believe I'm no better than you are—because I've stood by in silence while you polluted my 'ouse with your immoralities—because I've accepted from you the money you've made by preying on our poor soldiers that's fighting to protect our country from the 'Un. But you won't . . . (*There is a suggestion of tears of mortification in her voice.*)

MYRA

Oh, shut up—shut up! (*She is looking about the room to see if everything is there, and paying little attention to* MRS. HOBLEY.)

MRS. HOBLEY

I won't shut up. It's a grievous shame when a decent person is reduced to struggling for 'er rights with scum like you. God 'imself knows I've been patient with you.

MYRA

Is that so? (*Merely a polite question.*)

Mrs. Hobley

But I can tell you my patience is out. It's time you learned that I'm not conducting this 'ouse as a charitable institution for you and your kind.

Myra

It looks to me as though this room hasn't been occupied much lately.

Mrs. Hobley

Well—what if it 'asn't?

Myra

And yet you've got the nerve to raise the rent on me.

Mrs. Hobley

It's no more than I deserve for tolerating you at all.

Myra

Oh—I see! That extra eight shillings is hush money for your conscience.

Mrs. Hobley

I don't understand you.

Myra

You don't have to. You'll get paid. That's all you need to know.

MRS. HOBLEY

I'll see to that! Where is 'e—this friend of yours?

MYRA

He's down below, in the fish-and-chip shop. They let him in to get some food.

MRS. HOBLEY

What is 'e—a soldier?

MYRA

Yes.

MRS. HOBLEY

'Ow much money 'as 'e?

MYRA

How should I know? I haven't searched him.

MRS. HOBLEY

I'll just 'ave a look at 'im before I decide if 'e's good for the twenty-two bob.

MYRA

I don't want you to look at him. I want you to get out.

MRS. HOBLEY

Oh? Is there anything queer about him?

Myra

Say—why do you have to stay here? Why
don't you get down into the cellar? Don't you
know there's an air raid?

Mrs. Hobley

I 'ave other things than the German bombers
to protect myself against. If my poor, gallant
'usband were 'ere . . .

Myra

It won't do you any good to be so damned sus-
picious. Don't you think I'm able to get twenty-
two shillings?

Mrs. Hobley

You don't even know 'e 'as that much.

Myra

He's only just started his leave. He's got all
his pay.

Mrs. Hobley

Per'aps 'e 'as sense enough to keep it.

Myra

I tell you I'll get it out of him. You can leave
that to me.

Mrs. Hobley

You'd jolly well better, or you'll put on your
'at and coat and . . .

MYRA

Be quiet!

(*She has heard footsteps on the stairs outside. She goes to the door and calls, sweetly, "Is that you, soldier?"* ROY's *voice is heard, saying, "Yes —that kid told me to come up this way."* MYRA *says, "Come right in."*)

(ROY *comes in, carrying the suitcase and three packages, wrapped with newspaper.*)

ROY

Well—I couldn't get much. (*He looks around the room. He is embarrassed and sheeplishly ill at ease.*)

MRS. HOBLEY (*more agreeable*)

Good evening.

ROY

How de do.

MYRA

This is Mrs. Hobley, the landlady.

ROY

Very glad to know you, Mrs. Hobley. (*He comes forward to shake hands.*)

MRS. HOBLEY (*inspecting him with approval*)

Maple leafs! A Canadian.

Roy

Yes, ma'am. (*To* Myra) There's some tea there. But they didn't have any milk.

Mrs. Hobley

Been on leave a long time?

Roy

No—I just got out of hospital in Richmond to-day.

Mrs. Hobley

Oh—I see! Isn't that lovely! 'Out of 'ospital, your time's your own, lots of money—you *are* in luck.

Roy

I certainly am.

Myra

I think I heard somebody calling you downstairs, Mrs. Hobley.

Mrs. Hobley

No doubt you did, my dear. Well—I'll be saying good night. (*To* Roy) It's always a pleasure to 'ave any of the Canadians with us. We owe you such a debt for all you've done . . .

Roy (*with another sheepish laugh*)

There's lots of people over here who say different.

MRS. HOBLEY

And I 'ope you'll be very 'appy, on your leave.
(*To* MYRA) Good night, my dear. (*She pats*
MYRA's *cheek and goes out.*)

ROY

She's certainly very cordial.

MYRA

Yes. . . . What have you got here? (*She
starts to open the greasy parcels.*)

ROY

Well—that's fish and chips, and there's some
bread and margarine in here, and this is the tea.
It's a pretty punk meal, but . . .

MYRA

Oh, it looks fine. . . . I think there's a kettle
here some place.

(*She goes to a curtained wardrobe at the left
and takes from it a kettle, teapot and cups and
plates. She fills the kettle from the pitcher on
the wash-stand and puts it to boil on a gas heater,
but discovers that there is no gas. All this goes
on during the subsequent dialogue.*)

ROY

I was lucky to get anything. There wasn't a
soul in that tea-room except a little boy . . .

MYRA

Oh—that was Halbert Hedward. He's a great friend of mine.

ROY

All the rest were down in the cellar, but he'd sneaked upstairs. He said he was on guard in case the Germans got in.

MYRA

Oh, he's cute. After the raid's over he'll be out all night scouring the streets for pieces of shrapnel.

ROY

Souvenirs, eh? . . .

MYRA

No, he takes all the pieces he finds down to the war office and turns them in. He thinks they can use them a second time.

ROY

Maybe they do at that. Can't I help with any of that?

MYRA

Well—yes—you could, if you've got such a thing as a shilling about you.

ROY (*reaching in his pants pocket*)

Why, sure, I guess I can dig that up. . . .

Here. . . . (*He holds out a handful of coins. She takes a shilling.*)

MYRA

Thanks. (*She pats his hand, then puts the coin in the meter.*)

ROY

Say—what is that—a slot machine?

MYRA

It turns on the gas.

ROY

I thought maybe you were getting a package of gum.

MYRA

Oh—nothing like that. . . . Now don't forget to remind me to pay you back that shilling.

ROY

I think we can let that go. I'm giving this party, even the gas.

MYRA

You're a regular spendthrift, aren't you?

ROY

Well—I feel like one, now. I feel as if I've got so much money I could buy the whole town.

MYRA

Oh! I suppose you've got a lot of back pay.

Roy

Yes—you see they hold out on you while you're in hospital. That means it's been piling up.

Myra

How lovely—for you.

Roy

Well—I'm certainly going to try to have a good time with it.

Myra

I hope you don't go and lose it all—gambling, or anything like that.

Roy

Oh, don't worry. I wasn't born the day before yesterday.

Myra

No?

Roy (*happily*)

Now you're trying to kid me.

Myra (*putting her hand on his arm*)

Who says I was trying to do anything like that?

Roy

That's all right. You just go ahead and kid me all you want.

Myra (*slyly*)

Maybe I couldn't. (*She turns away to the kettle.*)

Roy (*fervently*)

Gee—it's great being here! I'm certainly grateful to old Heinie for putting on this show for me to-night. (*He wanders over to the window.*) It'll give me one more thing to brag about when I get home. (*He raises the window shade to look out.*) Gosh! You can see the flashes of the Ac-Acs . . .

(MYRA *darts across and pulls down the shade.*)

MYRA

Are you crazy?

Roy

Oh—I'm sorry. I keep forgetting about it being a war.

(*She goes back to the wash-stand to resume her work.*)

MYRA

If you pull that shade up any more, the cops will be around here to remind you.

Roy (*fondly*)

Cops! How long has it been since I've heard that word!

MYRA

They wear funny hats over here—but they're just as tough as the cops at home.

Roy

Would they mind if I smoked?

MYRA

No—I guess that'll be allowed.

(*He unbuttons one of the pockets of his tunic and takes out a pack of Camels.*)

ROY

Will you have one?

MYRA

No, thanks.

ROY

You don't smoke? (*He is beginning to feel more at ease.*)

MYRA

Yes—sometimes.

ROY

A lot of girls smoke now. In the hospitals, the V. A. D.'s were always sneaking cigarettes with us patients.

MYRA

Well, you can't blame 'em. Those nurses don't have much fun.

(*Roy has lit the cigarette and is watching her as she bustles back and forth across the stage, busy with her preparations.*)

ROY

Gee—it does me good to hear your voice.

MYRA

You've said that before.

Roy

I know—but when I hear you talk, I can't
seem to believe it.

Myra

Why not?

Roy

Well—you don't seem to fit in this town, with
bobbies and pubs and air-raids and all that . . .

Myra

I should think you'd be accustomed to hearing
a lot of American accents in the Canadian army.
They talk just like we do.

Roy

Sure—but the difference is, you're a woman.
That's what makes it so funny. I haven't heard
a woman talk like you since I came over in '14.

Myra

Fourteen? Were you here that quick?

Roy

Yes—but it was kind of an accident, though.

Myra

How'd you happen to do it?

Roy

You mean enlist?—Well—how did anybody
happen to do it? I was on the way home from
summer camp, and I stopped off in Toronto. That
was in August. The town was war crazy then.
Things were just getting going. The old con-
temptibles were on the retreat from Mons to the
Marne, and the recruiting officers were shouting
their heads off. Everybody was excited—it was
just like getting drunk, I guess.

Myra

I remember how it was here.

Roy

I was trying to elbow my way through the
crowd when a military band came down the street.
They were playing "It's A Long Way To Tip-
perary." The next thing I knew I was hot-footing
it up a gang-plank.

Myra

I guess it was that way with most.

Roy

Sure it was—just boyish enthusiasm.

Myra

And has it lasted?

Roy

What?

MYRA

The boyish enthusiasm.

ROY

For three years? *No*—you don't stay boyish very long in this war.

MYRA (*smiling*)

I can see that. . . . Are you getting hungry?

ROY

You bet I am.

MYRA

Then why don't you begin on the fish and chips?

ROY

I'd rather wait 'till you sit down.

MYRA

All right. (*She starts to draw chairs up to the table but he does it for her.*)

ROY

Say—you don't even know my name.

MYRA

No. What is it?

ROY

It's Roy Cronin. Lance Corporal Roy Cronin. Lance Corporal. That's a hot title, isn't it? What's your name?

MYRA

Myra.

ROY

Myra. Is that all?

MYRA

My last name's Deauville.

ROY

That sounds French. Are you of French descent?

MYRA

No. Deauville's just my stage name.

ROY

Oh, I see. What's your real name?

MYRA

I don't use that any more. . . . Stop watching the kettle. You keep it from boiling by watching it.

ROY

I wasn't watching the kettle. I was looking at you.

MYRA

You must be hard up for something to look at.

ROY

Believe me, I am!

MYRA

Hey, listen—*that* wasn't the right thing to say.

ROY

Oh, gosh! I guess I've forgotten how to be polite. But anyway, I think you're wonderful looking.

MYRA

I am not. I look like a tramp.

ROY

Now you're just fishing for compliments.

MYRA

No, soldier. . . . What did you say your name was?

ROY

Roy Cronin. Roy to you.

MYRA

Now we can begin to eat. (*She takes the kettle off. He jumps up.*)

ROY

Here—let me take that.

MYRA

There isn't much in the way of china and silverware here.

Roy

Well—fingers were invented before forks.   (*He laughs.*)

Myra

Do you take sugar?

Roy

Sure.

Myra

Well, there isn't any. Wait a minute.   (*She goes to her handbag, opens it, and takes from it a small bottle of saccharine pills.*)   Here's some saccharine.

Roy

How many of these pills make a lump of sugar?

Myra

One will be plenty. . . . I guess you're pretty sick of tea.

(*There is one cup and one glass for the tea. She fills the cup and hands it to him.*)

Roy (*as she pours*)

Yes! I wonder why nobody ever told these people over here about there being such a thing as coffee. . . . No—you take the cup and give me the glass.

Myra

No—you keep it. The saccharine is in the cup. I don't take it sweet.

Roy

Can't you get sugar?

Myra

I should say not. You can't get much of anything in London that ain't imitation. All the butter is margarine, and the eggs come in powder, and as for the meat . . .

Roy

Horse, I suppose.

Myra

Not even horse. There just ain't any. However, there's always Brussels sprouts.

Roy

Gosh! You have to join the army to get anything to eat.

Myra

I guess that's about it.

Roy (*his mouth full*)

The submarines must be pretty bad.

Myra

What did you say?

Roy

I said—the submarines must be getting pretty bad.

Myra

Yes. They seem to be a lot worse than the papers let on. Anyway, the food ships don't get by 'em.

Roy

Why do you stay here? Why didn't you go home long ago?

Myra

Oh—there's lots of reasons for that.

Roy

Don't you want to go home?

Myra

Of course I'd like to.

Roy

Then what's kept you back? Believe me—if it wasn't for the duration of this war, I'd be in Locke's Falls this minute.

Myra

Well, if you must know—I've stayed here because I never had the price of a ticket home.

Roy

Did the show close and leave you stranded?

Myra

Oh, no. We were a big success. But I got into another show, a kind of music hall thing. It went out into the provinces and died there.

Roy

It must have been a tough life, all right.

Myra

It was.

(*A machine-gun can be heard popping.*)

Roy

Listen! Machine-guns!

(Roy *goes to the window to listen.*)

Myra

They've got 'em set up on roofs all over the city.

Roy

Say—I can hear the German plane. Do you hear that—rmm, rmmm, rmmm? He must be flying awful low.

Myra

Well, don't open the window to wave to him.

(*There is a loud crash of a bomb in the near vicinity. They both jump.*)

Roy

Gosh! *That* wasn't any too far off. . . . Do you think it's safe for you to stay in here?

Myra

The roof keeps out the shrapnel. As for the bombs . . .

Roy

Oh—if one of *them* got a direct hit it wouldn't do us any good to be down in the cellar. (*The machine-gun has stopped firing.*) I guess he's gone somewhere else. (*He comes back to the table.*) You've got to hand it to those Heinies— flying hundreds of miles over here in the night just for the sake of dropping a few bombs and scaring people.

MYRA

They must be pretty brave.

ROY

Oh—they're brave all right. . . . It must be a thrill to be up there, looking down on London. . . . But I'd rather be right where I am. . . . (*He sits down and resumes his eating.*) You know, I've always wondered about chorus girls.

MYRA

What about them?

ROY

How much salary they got, and so forth.

MYRA

We were lucky to pull down four quid a week over here. That's about twenty dollars.

ROY

That's awful. And it was hard work, too, I'll bet.

MYRA

It was no cinch.

Roy

How did you ever learn all those dances?

Myra

Oh—just rehearsed and rehearsed.

Roy (*after a moment's pause*)

When you were on the stage, did you use to be chased a lot by men?

Myra

Not so much as people think.

Roy

I'll bet if I'd ever come around to the stage door you wouldn't even have looked at me.

Myra

Did you ever spend much time around stage doors?

Roy

No—I only went to the theatre a few times in my life, mostly in Syracuse.

Myra

What did you do for a living?

Roy

Oh, I fooled around a machine-shop. I was just headed for technical school when I got into this outfit.

MYRA

What did you do evenings?

ROY

I used to be mostly at the "Y."

MYRA

The what?

ROY

The "Y"—you know, the Y. M. C. A. I was a volunteer physical director.

MYRA

So you're a Y. M. C. A. boy.

ROY

You think that's the same as being a sissy, don't you?

MYRA

No, I wasn't thinking that.

ROY

Oh, a lot of people kid about the "Y," but I always liked working there. It keeps you in good physical condition.

MYRA

You're pretty healthy, aren't you?

ROY

Not now. You've got to remember I've been in hospital over eight months, and I've dropped quite a lot of weight. But it won't take me long to get back into shape.

MYRA

When do you have to go back to the army?

ROY

I've got fourteen days' sick leave. Then I report at Bramshott Camp. . . . I wish you'd tell me what kind of war work you've been doing.

MYRA

It wasn't anything interesting.

ROY

What was it—entertainment?

MYRA (*disturbed*)

What do you mean, entertainment?

ROY

I mean—amusing the troops. Lots of stage people have been doing that, putting on shows at the camps and the rest villages in France.

MYRA

Oh, no—I never did any of that. I've been a farmerette.

ROY

What the heck is a farmerette?

MYRA

What does it sound like? It's a girl that works on a farm.

Roy

That's a funny thing for you to do. Where did you ever learn anything about farming?

Myra

No place. But it was the only job they'd give me. I didn't have brains enough, I guess, to be even an assistant trained nurse. They were advertising for women recruits—for the Waacs, and all those things. That was last spring, just when the U. S. got into the war.

Roy

And you joined up?

Myra

Yes, I was like you. I suddenly got patriotic and went down to the office in Whitehall, and the next thing *I* knew they'd put me to work with a hoe.

Roy

That took a lot of nerve, all right. . . . What made you quit?

Myra

The farming season is over and most of us were laid up for the winter.

Roy

What do you expect to do now?

MYRA

I haven't made up my mind. . . . Want some more tea?

ROY

Thanks. This certainly isn't much of a meal, but it was the best I could get.

MYRA

After you've been around London a couple of weeks you'll consider this a banquet.

ROY

I hadn't planned to stay the whole fourteen days in London.

MYRA

Oh! Have you friends you can visit?

ROY

No—there's not a soul I know over here. But I thought I'd like to take a little trip.

MYRA

Where'd you plan to go?

ROY

Well, I thought I'd like to go up to Birmingham and see what it's like there. And then I promised my family I wouldn't miss the chance to visit Shakespeare's birthplace.

MYRA

That's very interesting.

Roy

Ever been there?

Myra

No, but I've heard lots about it.

Roy

Maybe now I'll decide not to take the trip.

Myra

Why not?

Roy

I think I'd have a better time staying here in London.

Myra

You oughtn't to miss the trip.
(*They have finished eating by now.*)

Roy

I can take that some other time. What I'd like to do on this leave is see a lot of you. . . . Would you like to go out with me? I mean to shows and things like that?

Myra

Why, yes—sure—of course I would. But you can find lots better things to do than that.

Roy

I don't think so. Going around with you would be my idea of a good time. It would be something to look back to!

Myra

Would it?

ROY

You bet it would!

MYRA

Well, I'm sure I appreciate it. . . . Here—I'll clean this stuff out of here.

ROY

Let me do it.

MYRA

No—you sit still. (*She gathers up the dishes.*) I'll just put them in the sink outside.

(ROY *holds the door open for her as she goes out. . . . He looks around the room, goes to the window, peaks out, then ambles over to the gramophone. He examines the record, and then starts it going. He sits down on the bed to listen. After a while* MYRA *comes in.*)

ROY

Listen to what it's playing.

MYRA

Yes—that's Hazel Dawn's number.

ROY

Gosh—how that takes me back.

MYRA

Me too. (*She sits down beside him.*)

ROY

That was certainly a great show.

MYRA

Yes.

ROY

That's a show I'd like to seé again—with you in it.

MYRA

You wouldn't even notice me in it.

ROY

I wouldn't notice anything else.

MYRA

You're getting easier with your compliments.

ROY

That wasn't any compliment. I really meant it. I think you're a peach. . . . It was pretty lucky, wasn't it, our meeting like that in the middle of an air raid?

MYRA

Yes, it was.

ROY

I mean—two people from the same country, from the same *state*, with the same ideas about things.

MYRA

Do you think we've got the same ideas about things?

ROY

Of course we have.

MYRA

What makes you think that, Roy?

Roy

Gee—I like to hear you call me by my name.

Myra

What would I call you by?

Roy

Well—in the army—you usually get called by just your last name, or your number.

Myra

But what makes you think we've got the same ideas?

Roy

We talk the same language, don't we?

Myra

Yes, but that doesn't mean much. It doesn't change the fact that you're a Y. M. C. A. boy. . . .

Roy

Oh, lay off that.

Myra

Well, you are. And I'm a—an ex-chorus girl.

Roy

That don't worry me.

Myra

What don't?

Roy

Your having been in the chorus. I know you're all right.

MYRA

How do you know it?

ROY

I can just tell

MYRA

That's no answer.

ROY

Well—what you did—I mean volunteering for that farm work. That was a pretty fine thing to do.

MYRA

And I can just tell you're all right yourself.

ROY

There—you see—we have got the same ideas.
(*Whenever the gramophone record runs out,* MYRA *shuts off the machine.*)

MYRA

I guess I'd like to have a smoke, now.

ROY

Oh, sure. Excuse me. (*He hands her the pack of Camels.*)

MYRA

Where'd you get those?

ROY

In a parcel from home.

MYRA

I haven't seen any of those since I don't know when.

ROY (*lighting the cigarette for her*)

It'll probably taste terrible at first, after you've got used to English cigarettes. Do you inhale?

MYRA

Certainly.

ROY

Girls don't usually inhale. They just puff.

MYRA

I'll bet you don't like to see girls smoke.

ROY

Well—I don't like it usually, to tell you the truth. But it seems to be different with you. Everything's different with you.

(*She sits down. He has been looking about for the ash-tray. Having found it, he has set it down on the table beside her.*)

MYRA

Roy . . . do you get many parcels from home?

ROY

Oh, sure—the family send me cake and candy and cigarettes and wristlets and things like that. Say—what are you supposed to do with wristlets, anyway?

MYRA

You wear them, don't you?

ROY

I guess so, but I couldn't ever figure out why.
(*He sits down, awkwardly, on the edge of the
table.*)

MYRA

What's your family like, Roy?

ROY

Oh, I don't know. They're just like any other
family, I guess. Only there's more of them. I've
got more near relatives than I know what to do
with.

MYRA

Any children of your own?

ROY

Gosh, no. I'm not married.

MYRA

Oh! Does all your family live in Locke's Falls?

ROY

In it or near it.

MYRA

It must be very nice.

ROY

Yes—in a way. You know, you sometimes get

sick of having so many relatives. But it's a lot of fun around Christmas. The whole family goes broke on account of the number of presents we have to give to each other.

MYRA

And I'll bet you have big dinners at Thanksgiving.

ROY

Oh—don't speak of it. I was thinking of that only this afternoon. It must be just about Thanksgiving Day now.

MYRA

They don't celebrate it here.

ROY

I'll say they don't. They've got nothing to celebrate it with. Say—do you suppose there'd be any chance of us buying a turkey in this town?

MYRA

A turkey! You might just as well go down to the Tower and ask them to hand you over the crown jewels.

(*She goes over to the right with the remains of the bread.*)

ROY

Do you know what I'd like to be doing? I'd like to be eating a big Thanksgiving dinner, with you. . . . (*He follows her across.*)

MYRA

Is that an invitation?

ROY

And then I'd like to be taking you out to see
the Penn-Cornell game. But probably Penn and
Cornell aren't playing this year, on account of
the U. S. being in the war. (*The machine-gun is
heard popping. He goes to the window.*) There
goes that Vickers again. . . . Talk about at-
tracting Heinie's attention—those machine-gun-
ners are liable to make this district unpopular.

MYRA

I should think that'd sound terrible to you—
on account of having been hit with one . . .

ROY

Well—I don't know . . .
(*He is at the left. She crosses so that she is
close to him.*)

MYRA

They won't ever send you back to the trenches,
will they?

ROY

They won't, eh! Say! They'll shoot me up the
line so fast I'll bump into the parapet.

MYRA

You'd think, with all the time you've been in the
army, and then getting wounded, you'd think

they'd have some consideration on you, and give you a safe job.

Roy

They've got plenty of consideration—but the trouble is, they haven't got plenty of men. (*There is the barest suggestion of bravado in his tone as he says this.*)

Myra

How will you feel when you get back there?

Roy

Just the way I did before, I guess. I'll just sit around and pray for another flesh wound.

Myra

Was it just a flesh wound that kept you in hospital for over eight months?

Roy

Not exactly. It tore away some of the bone in the shoulder.

Myra

How'd they ever fix you up?

Roy

Oh, they kept on operating until I could begin working my arm all right. (*He moves his right arm by way of demonstration.*) The fellers in the ward used to kid me about it. They said the medical officers were running a regular bus service between my cot and the pictures.

MYRA

The pictures?

ROY

That's what they called the operating-room—
because it had rows of seats in it, like a movie
theatre.

(*He sits down on the arm of a chair at the left.*)

MYRA

That must have hurt an awful lot.

ROY

I ought to tell you it didn't hurt at all. But I
like to hear you sympathize with me.

(MYRA *sits down close to him.*)

MYRA

Does it do you any good to get sympathy out
of me?

ROY

It does me good just to look at you, Myra.
Just being here and . . .

MYRA

That's the first time you've said *my* name.

ROY

I know it. I didn't have the nerve to before.

MYRA

You know something, Roy?

ROY

What?

MYRA

I don't think you've ever gone around much
with girls.

ROY

What makes you think that?

MYRA

The way you talk to me.

ROY

Well, of course, when you're in the army you
don't have much chance to go out with girls. (*He
slides down from the arm of the chair into the
chair itself.*)

MYRA

How about when you're on leave?

ROY

There's not much chance even then—I mean,
with decent girls. Take a feller like me, for in-
stance, in a strange country—how would I meet
any decent girls?

MYRA

I suppose not.

ROY

It took an air raid and a freak of luck to fix it
up for me to meet you.

MYRA

Do you think—would you call me a decent girl?

ROY

I wouldn't put you in the same class with other girls.

MYRA

Why not?

ROY

Well—you're nice.

(*The sounds of the barrage, which have been occasionally audible throughout this scene, have stopped entirely by now. A few shrill whistle blasts are heard from various distances, but* ROY *and* MYRA *are paying no attention to them.*)

MYRA

After you go back to the trenches, Roy—I'd like to send you some parcels.

ROY

Gee—that would be great.

MYRA

I'd like to make something for you—socks, or something like that.

ROY

I can always use socks. And anyway—whatever you sent me, I'd treasure it.

MYRA

I'd just like to think there was something to make you think—to remind you of our little meeting.

ROY

I don't need anything to remind me, Myra. I'm not likely to forget—anything about you. . . . You can't imagine what it is—how it feels to find someone, here, that's friendly . . .

MYRA

I guess I can imagine that. . . .

(*There is a discreet tap at the door.* MYRA *is startled.*)

MYRA

Who's that?

MRS. HOBLEY (*from outside*)

It's me, dear—Mrs. 'Obley.

MYRA

Well?

MRS. HOBLEY

I just thought you'd like to know they're sounding the "all clear" in the streets.

MYRA

Oh—thanks.

MRS. HOBLEY

I'll be going to bed now, dear.

MYRA

All right.

MRS. HOBLEY

Did you want to see me about anything to-night?

MYRA

Not now, Mrs. Hobley. I'll see you in the morning.

MRS. HOBLEY

Oh! Then good night. Sleep well.

MYRA

Good night.

ROY

She's a good soul, that Mrs. Hobley.

MYRA

Yes— she's a love. (*She has gone back to the dresser and looked at* MRS. HOBLEY's *bill.*)

ROY

She seems to take a great interest in you. (*He notices that there is something on her mind.*) What's the matter?

MYRA (*coming down*)

Did you hear what she said? The raid's over.

ROY

That's fine.

Myra

It's all right to go out into the streets now.

Roy

That sounds like a hint to me to buzz off.

Myra

Well—it's pretty late—and I guess you'll be wanting to get to bed. I mean, you probably aren't accustomed to staying up so late on account of being in hospital so long. (*She has picked up his haversack and his cap and is handing them to him.*)

Roy

Say—all I've done since last April is go to bed. (*He puts on the haversack with poorly disguised reluctance.*)

Myra

You need plenty of rest.

Roy

I guess you need it more than I do.

Myra

Well—good night, Roy.

Roy

Good night. (*He goes to the left, obviously hurt by the abruptness of this dismissal.*)

Myra

Where were you expecting to go—to-night? (*She follows him to the door.*)

ROY (*at the door*)

Well—I had thought I'd drop around to the Beaver Hut. That's the Canadian Y. M. C. A.

MYRA

Do they have beds there?

ROY

A few beds, and plenty of floor space.

MYRA

I hope they make you comfortable.

ROY

Oh, I'll get fixed up.

MYRA

Well—it certainly has been nice seeing you . . .

ROY

It certainly has. (*They shake hands. His enthusiasm has been refreshed by the warmth of her farewell.*)

MYRA

I've had a great time talking to you.

ROY

So've I. It's wonderful to be able to just sit around and not have to *do* anything.

MYRA

Yes, it's wonderful, for a change. (*She turns away.*)

Roy

Well—to-morrow we'll go some place for lunch and I'll get tickets for a show, anything you suggest . . .

Myra

Listen, Roy . . .

Roy

What?

Myra

I think we'd better say good-by here and now.

Roy

Good-by? But I'm going to see you . . .

Myra

I won't be able to meet you to-morrow, after all. (*She walks away from him. He follows her.*)

Roy

Why not, for Pete's sake?

Myra

I'll be very busy.

Roy

Busy with what?

Myra

I've got to get back to work.

Roy

But you've been working for a long time, on that farm. You're set for a vacation!

MYRA

No—that sounds good, but I've got to get a job right away.

ROY

On the stage?

MYRA

Well—any job I can get.

ROY

You mean, you need the money?

MYRA

That's about it.

ROY

Now look here—you just forget about money for the next couple of weeks. You let me take care of that part of it.

MYRA

I can't do that.

ROY

Certainly you can. I've got more money than I know what to do with. I've got over seven pounds in my pocket this minute, and there's more waiting for me at the pay-corps office. Why, I'm rich. And I'd like to know how I could spend it to better advantage than going around with you.

MYRA

That's very kind of you, Roy. But just the

same, I'd better get back to work. I'm not going
to let you spend everything you've got . . .

Roy

I know what you're thinking. You don't want
to put yourself in the position of being indebted
to me or anybody else. Well, you won't be. I'll
be the one whose indebted to you.

Myra

I'd like to give you some advice, Roy.

Roy

If it's to invest my money in government
bonds, I don't want to hear it.

Myra

No—I've been thinking it over, and I think
you'd better be starting on your trip to-morrow.

Roy

My *trip?*

Myra

To Shakespeare's home, and all those places.

Roy

Oh, to hell with—I'd rather stay here.

Myra

You'd better get out of this town just as quick
as you can.

Roy

What's the matter with it?

MYRA

It isn't healthy.

ROY

Is there a plague here, or something?

MYRA

It just isn't wholesome for you, Roy. You're a soldier . . .

ROY

Well, who isn't?

MYRA

There's only two things for a soldier to do here—that is, when he's a stranger, like you. . . . . Drink—and—and get himself mixed up with dirty women.

ROY

Oh, that's bunk. Just because a lot of the troops run wild when they get into the big city. That's because they've got no friends. But you see, I've got you. Why, there's lots of things we can do. We can visit all the places of historical interest. There's any number of 'em here. . . . Anyway, that trip of mine is off. Forget it— and forget about money, too. (*He turns and goes to the left.*) I'll be around in the morning.

MYRA

What time?

Roy (*again at the door*)

Any time you say.

Myra

Well—you better not come before noon.

Roy

Want to sleep late, eh?

Myra

Yes.

Roy

It'll do you good. I'll kill time somehow or other until noon. . . . Well, good night.

Myra

Good night, Roy.

Roy

I left those Camels on the table. I thought you might like to have one in the morning.

Myra

Oh—thanks.

Roy

It certainly has been a lot of fun.

Myra

It certainly has. (*He stares at her a few moments.*)

Roy

Would you feel offended if I asked for a little kiss?

MYRA

No,—I—go ahead. (*Her head is lowered. He bends down and kisses her cheek.*)

ROY

Gosh! That was kind of embarrassing, wasn't it?

MYRA

Yes—it was.

ROY

But it was all right, though. . . . Well,—see you to-morrow.

MYRA

Sure.

(*He goes out. Still smiling,* MYRA *saunters back to the dresser, picks up the bill* MRS. HOB-*ley had left there, looks at it and tosses it down. She regards herself for a moment in the mirror. Then she puts on her hat and coat, opens her trunk and takes from it a shabby white fox fur neckpiece, which she throws about her shoulders. She applies powder to her nose and rouge to her cheeks and lips. She notices the package of Camels and is about to put them into her hand-bag, but she changes her mind and replaces them on the table. She goes to the door, switching out the lights as she does so. She opens the door and goes out.*)

CURTAIN

ACT II

ACT II

SCENE I

MYRA's *room is just as it was at the end of Act I. The lamp is burning low, the shades are down, but the noonday sun is streaming in through the cracks between the shade and the window frame.*

MRS. HOBLEY *comes in, and sniffs distastefully; the stuffiness of the unaired room oppresses her.*

She turns out the light, lifts the shade, puts up the window, does a little straightening up and smoothing the bed, and perhaps gives a few flicks here and there with the dust rag. She approaches the gramophone as though she were going to play it, and then decides not to.

There is a sharp knock on the door, but before MRS. HOBLEY *has had a chance to say "Come in," the* MILITARY POLICEMAN *enters.* MRS. HOBLEY *is startled at sight of him.*

MILITARY POLICEMAN

Morning, Mrs. 'Obley. I was told I'd find you on this floor.

MRS. HOBLEY

What—what are you doing 'ere?

101

MILITARY POLICEMAN

My duty, as always.

MRS. HOBLEY (*brusquely*)

Well, you can be off with it, then. The military police 'as no duties in my 'ouse—I can promise you that.

MILITARY POLICEMAN (*unperturbed*)

Orders from 'eadquarters is that we're to go through all the lodging 'ouses in this area and inspect passes of all soldiers found therein.

MRS. HOBLEY

Soldiers! You know perfectly well there's no soldiers lodging in this 'ouse.

MILITARY POLICEMAN

Quite so. But you 'ave other lodgers 'ere, and soldiers are apt to come in, to call. You know what a sociable lot soldiers are.

MRS. HOBLEY (*resuming her work*)

Well, you may look to your 'eart's content, but you'll find no troops 'ere.

MILITARY POLICEMAN

Who's occupying this room now?

MRS. HOBLEY (*exasperated*)

By whose authority are you annoying me?

MILITARY POLICEMAN

By authority of the King, ma'am. 'E takes a great interest in the doings of all 'is subjects, even the 'umblest. . . . Come along, now. It won't 'urt you to tell me what I 'ave to know.

MRS. HOBLEY

It's that little one—calls 'erself Myra Deauville.

(*The* MILITARY POLICEMAN *has taken a note-book and pencil from his pocket.*)

MILITARY POLICEMAN (*writing*)

Myra. . . . 'Ow do you spell that last?

MRS. HOBLEY

D-E-A-U-V-I-L.

MILITARY POLICEMAN

Age?

MRS. HOBLEY

I don't know—twenty-five to thirty.

MILITARY POLICEMAN

That's close enough. . . . Profession?

MRS. HOBLEY

Yes.

MILITARY POLICEMAN

I see. . . . Myra Deauville. . . . I don't think I know 'er.

MRS. HOBLEY

She's American.

MILITARY POLICEMAN

Oh, *is* she! (*He makes a note of that.*) Strange I don't know 'er. 'Ow long 'as she been 'ere?

MRS. HOBLEY

She's just come back, last night. Been away for months, on a farm.

MILITARY POLICEMAN

I'll look 'er up later. I like to keep tabs on all of 'em.

MRS. HOBLEY

Huh! You must 'ave your 'ands full in these times.

MILITARY POLICEMAN

Well, it *is* a task. It's got so now you can't discriminate between the ~~tarts~~ *indecent* and the decent girls, and vice versa.

MRS. HOBLEY (*emphatically*)

You can thank the war for that! Decency went out in 1914. But it'll come back; you mark my words!

MILITARY POLICEMAN

Of *course* it'll come back! In triumph! Even if you and me may not be 'ere to welcome it. 'Ave there been any soldiers in 'ere since last night?

MRS. HOBLEY (*reluctantly*)

There was one . . .

MILITARY POLICEMAN

Ah! Did you 'appen to notice what 'is regiment was?

MRS. HOBLEY

Canadian.

MILITARY POLICEMAN

Oh, Lord—one of those. They're the 'ardest for us to deal with. They 'ave no respect for authority. I often think, if those Canadians only 'ated the Bosches as much as they 'ate us M. P.'s, they'd be in Berlin by now. (*He goes toward the window.*) Do you know if Kitty's in her room?

MRS. HOBLEY

I know nothing about that vulgar person. She's no lodger of mine, thank 'eaven.

MILITARY POLICEMAN

Well, if you don't mind I'll go across the roof and see if she's got any of the army in 'er possession. . . . Good day, Mrs. 'Obley.

(*He goes out the window and off to the right.*)

MRS. HOBLEY

And good day to *you!*

(*She goes out the door at the left and comes bustling back, carrying the cups, plates and teapot which* MYRA *had left in the sink outside. She places them on the shelf in the wardrobe.* ROY *appears in the doorway. He is carrying a bunch of autumnal flowers, wrapped in damp newspaper.*)

Roy

Myra—it's me. . . . (*He sees* Mrs. Hobley.) Oh—excuse me—I thought . . .

Mrs. Hobley (*cordially*)

Come right in.

Roy (*coming in*)

Thanks.

Mrs. Hobley

I've just been doing a bit of dusting. I *do* like to 'ave things neat.

Roy

Where's Miss—Miss Deauville. (*The flossy name embarrasses him.*)

Mrs. Hobley

She's out somewhere—shopping, I expect. (*There is a note of scorn in this.*)

Roy

She told me to be here at noon—so I guess she'll be back before long.

(*He puts the flowers on the table.*)

Mrs. Hobley

I don't doubt she will.

Roy (*at the window*)

You certainly don't get much of a view here, do you?

Mrs. Hobley

You get sunlight and fresh air, when you want them. That's the main thing. They can 'ave their views.

Roy

Well—I know if *I* lived over here, I'd want to have a room that looked out over Westminster Abbey, or one of those places.

Mrs. Hobley

If I was you, I wouldn't stand too close to that window.

Roy (*laughing*)

What's the matter? Is the air-raid still on?

Mrs. Hobley

It's the Military Police.

Roy

The M. P.'s? Well, what's biting them?

Mrs. Hobley

They're looking for stray soldiers. There was one of em in 'ere just now. 'E went across that roof.

Roy

Well, he can't do anything to me. I've got my pass, and it's all regular, too.

Mrs. Hobley

Let us 'ope so. . . . Now, if you'll excuse me—I 'ave work to do . . .

ROY

Oh—sure. I guess it's all right for me to wait here?

MRS. HOBLEY

Yes, you can wait. (*She starts to go.*) When she comes in, tell 'er I'll want to see 'er . . .

ROY

Sure. I'll tell her that.

MRS. HOBLEY

'K you.

(MRS. HOBLEY *goes out. . . .* ROY *starts to whistle "They'll never believe me." He takes off his tunic, extracts his polishing kit from his haversack, and sits down.*

(*He then sets to work shining the brass buttons on his tunic, using a can of Brasso, button-stick, brush and flannel cloth in the process. It is a painstaking operation. As he works, his whistling changes to humming, and when he comes to the words, "And I'm certainly going to tell them," he sings them with great positiveness. He hears the sound of footsteps on the roof outside and looks up.* KITTY *appears at the window. She is startled to see him.*)

KITTY

Oh!

ROY

Where'd *you* come from?

KITTY

I didn't mean to intrude. Is Myra 'ome?

ROY

No—but she'll probably be here any minute.

KITTY (*about to depart*)

Well—I shan't disturb you.

ROY

You're not disturbing me. I just came in my-self.

KITTY

Oh—you *just* came in?

ROY

Yes. Was Myra expecting you?

KITTY

Yes—I told her I'd pop in this morning. I live in the next 'ouse. But I'll be toddling back. (*She disappears.*)

ROY (*at the window*)

That roof doesn't look like a very good place to do much toddling.

KITTY (*invisible*)

Oh—we go back and forth on it all the time.

ROY

If you want to wait for Myra, why don't you come in?

KITTY (*reappearing at the window*)
Do you mind?

ROY
Not at all.

KITTY (*roguishly*)
Then look the other way.

ROY
Oh, sure——

(KITTY *steps in over the low window-sill.*)

KITTY
It's all right to look now.

ROY
Sit right down.

KITTY
You're very kind.

ROY
I just thought I'd polish up the old brass while I was waiting. It's quite a job keeping it clean in this town.

KITTY
I expect you 'ave to give it quite a lot of attention.

ROY
Yes—they say shiny buttons will win the war.

KITTY
Do they?

Roy

Sure—they've been trying that theory for three years now, and so far as I can see, the war isn't won yet. Maybe it's time for 'em to try something else. (*He laughs.*)

Kitty

You *are* a joker!

Roy

They make us work for hours polishing these buttons, and then the minute we get in the line we have to smear 'em with lampblack so they won't make targets for Heinie to snipe at.

Kitty

It's an odd war, right enough.

Roy

You said it. "Odd" is just the word.

Kitty

You're a Canadian, aren't you?

Roy

Well, I'm with that army. I belong to the R. C. R.'s. They call us the Brasso Battalion— that's because we use so much of this stuff.

Kitty

We *do* admire the Canadians. They've done such 'eroic work.

Roy

They're good troops, all right.

KITTY

We're proud of you, 'ere in the old country. Sons of the Empire—that's what we call the Canadians, and Australians, too.

ROY

The Australians are over-rated. They make a lot of noise and show off—but when it comes to proving anything in the line, well, they're a lot of false alarms, if you ask me.

KITTY

I agree perfectly.

ROY

Understand that I'm not a Canadian myself.

KITTY

No?

ROY

I'm an American.

KITTY

An *American!* 'Ow fascinating!

ROY

Twenty-five per cent of the Canadian army are Americans. We're not Sons of the Empire at all. We're kind of red-headed step-children.

KITTY

All the more credit to you, I'm sure. . . . I suppose you saw the raid, last night?

(KITTY *is not particularly interested in this guest of* MYRA'S, *but is trying hard to be sociable. . . . Later she begins to see the possibilities and to exploit them.*)

ROY

Well—I heard some of it.

KITTY

They're awful things, air raids. They really are dreadful. You've no idea what 'avoc they've raised. (*She looks out the window.*) We'll 'ave another to-night.

ROY

How do you know?

KITTY

Look at the weather. Not a cloud in the sky and the moon still at the full. It's rotten luck.

ROY

I should think it would make everbody kind of jumpy, knowing it's coming.

KITTY

We're accustomed to it, by now. We 'ave so much excitement 'ere. Between the 'Un airplanes, that keep us from sleeping, and the 'Un submarines, that keep us from eating, we're for it every which way.

ROY

I don't see why they have to drag in the civilians into the war.

KITTY

Oh, well—what's fair for the troops is fair for us. (*She notices the flowers.*) Where did these lovely flowers come from?

ROY

Oh—I brought those. I happened to be passing through Covent Garden market on the way over and I thought I might as well . . .

KITTY

They *are* sweet! Shall I put them in water?

ROY

Why—sure, would you?

(KITTY *puts them in the water pitcher on the wash-stand at the left.*)

KITTY

I expect you're an old friend of Myra's.

ROY

Well—yes. We're friends.

KITTY

You knew 'er in the States, per'aps?

ROY

No—I never knew her there.

KITTY

I see. Just a war-time acquaintance.

ROY

Yes—that's it. You a friend of Myra's, too?

KITTY

Oh, my, yes. We're the best. She and I used to work together.

ROY

Were you in "The Pink Lady" too?

KITTY

Oh, no—but we've been intimate for ever so long. It's strange she never mentioned you. She 'as so few friends.

ROY

Well, to tell you the truth, we only just met.

KITTY

This morning?

ROY

No, last night.

KITTY

Oh?

ROY

We sort of stumbled over each other during the air raid.

KITTY

That's odd—'cause I saw her after the raid ...

ROY

Oh, you did? Then you must have been in

here after I left. I hope she got a good rest. She
certainly was tired.

KITTY

Oh, yes—you're quite right. She was tired,
the poor ducky.

Roy (*earnestly*)

I hate to think of her going through all this—
air raids and bum food, and . . .

KITTY

I know—she's such a little thing.

Roy

What kind of a life does she lead, anyway?

KITTY

Oh—a miserable life.

Roy

How do you mean?

KITTY

Why—miserable—un'appy.

Roy

I guessed that. You know, it's hard for me to
find out much from her about herself. She doesn't
seem to want to talk about her own affairs. All
she does is ask me questions about the war—as
though I had anything to tell about that that

everybody hasn't heard a million times. How does she get along?

KITTY

It's a constant struggle.

ROY

You say she hasn't got many friends here?

KITTY

Oh, no. That's the 'ardest part of it. She's so *lonely*.

ROY

I'll bet she is. You can tell that just to look at her.

KITTY

She 'asn't a living soul to take care of 'er. No one she can count on for 'elp—and she does need it.

ROY

You can tell that, too.

KITTY

Of course, *I'm* devoted to 'er. But I'm poverty-stricken, myself. My dear 'usband is no more.

ROY

Oh—I'm sorry.

KITTY (*deliberately tearful*)

'E was a soldier—young and 'andsome and full

of 'ope, like yourself. 'E got 'is in the crater at Loos.

Roy

Poor feller. That was a nasty scrap.

Kitty

I 'elp Myra all I can—but what can *I* do?

Roy

How about Mrs. Hobley? She seems friendly.

Kitty

She *seems* friendly, yes. But Mrs. 'Obley is a proper whited sepluchre, I can promise you. She's 'ard 'earted, she is. Not that one can blame 'er. She 'as to live, like the rest of us. *'Er* 'usband's a prisoner in Germany, and all she gets is separation allowance—a few bob a week. You know —our Tommies aren't paid as 'andsomely as you Canadians.

Roy

I know—us Canadians are rich. We draw down all of a dollar a day—that's four shillings.

Kitty

That's four times what the Tommy is paid.

Roy

Did Myra get any salary while she was on that farm?

KITTY

Not a penny. She sacrificed 'erself 'eroically, she did.

ROY

But what's she going to do now? How will she support herself?

KITTY

I've wondered about that very thing. Jobs are scarce in London in these 'ard times.

ROY

She doesn't seem to be very crazy about going back on the stage.

KITTY

And quite right, too. The theatre's no place for a girl like 'er.

ROY

I guess it isn't a very pleasant atmosphere.

KITTY

A girl in Myra's position 'as no chance, unless . . .

ROY

Unless what?

KITTY

Well—it's always been my 'ope—you might almost call it my dream—that some day, some nice young man would come along and—and appreciate Myra.

ROY

Oh!

(ROY *turns away—but* KITTY *shrewdly sees that she has made her point, and she hastens to drive it home.*)

KITTY

And marry 'er, and give 'er a 'ome, and protect 'er.

ROY

I suppose there hasn't been much chance of that in the——the environment that she lives in.

KITTY

You've got it! And that's just the danger she's facing at this minute.

ROY

How do you mean, danger?

KITTY

Bad influences. You don't know what London is in war time. The immorality 'ere is ghastly.

ROY

I guess Myra can take care of herself on that.

KITTY

'Ow can she, if she's neglected and 'elpless and stony broke and face to face with starvation?

ROY

Is she broke?

KITTY

'Er condition is desperate—desperate, I tell you! An' if the young man I've been 'oping for don't pop up soon, 'e'll be *too late!* That's what 'e'll be.

ROY

I never thought it was so bad.

KITTY

Of course you didn't. You'd know nothing if you depended on 'er for information. She's too proud to breathe a word of complaint. That's so often the way with those who 'ave enjoyed better circumstances.

ROY

Did she used to be well off?

KITTY

Oh! Didn't you know of her family?

ROY

No—she never mentioned that she had any.

KITTY

That's like 'er. Why—she comes of one of the most aristocratic families in the States—one of the *old* families—although of course she goes incog.

ROY

Then that's why she wouldn't tell me her real name.

Kitty

Why—why, yes . . .

Roy

And do you mean to tell me her family have deserted her?

Kitty

I don't believe they know she's still alive. You see—there's 'er pride again! She'd die before she'd ask them for 'elp.

Roy

The poor kid.

(*He is genuinely moved.* Kitty *is intensely gratified to observe the extent of the progress she has made.*)

Kitty

Not that I 'ave any right to interfere. I know 'ow it is with those who interest themselves in other people's troubles. They may 'ave the best of intentions, but do they ever get any thanks for it? They do not. On the contrary, it's always, "Mind your *own* business." But for all of that, I just can't 'elp feeling sick with sympathy for that poor child—and she is no more than a child, knowing nothing of the world, nothing of the uglier side of life, plunging 'ead on to the depths of degradation.

Roy

Well, believe me, I'm thankful to you for telling me all this.

KITTY

You would be. You're a real man, with a big 'eart and a sense of decency. But 'ow many are there like you? 'Ow many are there would 'ave any interest in a girl other than her body? Next to none. You're in the army—you must know that.

ROY

I guess I do know it, all right. It isn't very nice to think about—but you've got to face facts.

KITTY

Unpleasant as they may be.

ROY

Look here—I've got an idea . . .

KITTY (*eagerly*)

Yes?

ROY

You seem to be real kind, and sympathetic.

KITTY

I'm no more than a fellow 'uman being.

ROY

I'd like to do something to fix it up for Myra. I'm pretty darn fond of her, and I . . .

KITTY

As who could 'elp but being.

Roy

I don't see any reason why you and I couldn't cook up a scheme that would . . .

Kitty

Hush!

(Myra *comes in. She is wearing the same tawdry fur piece that she had put on before going out the night before.*)

'Ullo, dear.

Myra

Oh—I didn't know anybody was here. (*She hastily takes off her hat and the white fox fur.*)

Kitty

I just stopped in, ducky, and found Mr.—ah—your friend. We've 'ad a jolly chat, 'aven't we?

(*While* Myra *is turned away,* Kitty *rapidly signals to* Roy *to leave.*)

Roy

Yes—I've been hearing all about the war . . .

Kitty

I've been doing my best to persuade the corporal to stay 'till you get back, but he seems to be . . .

Myra (*worried*)

Why—were you going some place, Roy?

(Kitty *signals to* Roy *to say "yes."*)

Roy

Yes—I've got to go out to . . .

Kitty

But he's promised to be back in a tick.

Roy

I thought I'd go down to the post office. I've got a money-order to get cashed.

Kitty

My! Fancy 'aving money orders!

Roy (*at the door*)

Oh—Mrs. Hobley told me to tell you she was anxious to see you.

Myra

Oh—thanks.

Roy

Will I tell her you're here?

Myra

No—I'll go right down and see her.

(Roy *glances toward* Kitty, *as though appealing to her to pave the way for him.* Kitty *nods to him, significantly. He goes out.*)

Myra (*accusingly*)

What've you been saying to him?

KITTY

Now, my dear, don't you worry about what
I . . .

MYRA

Have you been telling him anything?

KITTY

I've been telling 'im nothing that wasn't good
for 'im to 'ear. Of course, I 'ad to ask a few
tactful questions—but I soon found out what to
say.

MYRA

And what was that?

KITTY

I 'ymned your bloody praises! I slipped once,
but 'e didn't notice it.

MYRA

How'd you slip?

KITTY

I almost told 'im about seeing you last night,
after the raid. You know—that time in front of
Simpson's . . .

MYRA

What did he say?

KITTY

'E corrected me, bless 'is 'eart. . . . What'd
you do with that Army Service Corps bloke you
'ad in tow?

MYRA

I took him to the Silver Cross Hotel.

KITTY

What was he good for?

MYRA

Eight bob. After I got rid of him, I just fell asleep at the Silver Cross. I ain't been home since. I was hoping *he'd* come here and go away. (*The "he" refers to* ROY.)

KITTY

Not 'im. 'E waited to 'ear all the information I 'ad to give 'im about you.

MYRA (*with a suggestion of belligerence*)
And what was that?

KITTY

That you're a poor, maltreated little virgin, 'alf starved, and 'ungry for love.

MYRA

Thanks—but you didn't need to lie to him.

KITTY

Oh—is it a lie to say that you're 'ungry and poor?

MYRA

No—I meant the other part of it.

KITTY

Well, that didn't 'urt. . . . Oh, you *are* a lucky one. *Your* troubles will trouble you no more.

MYRA

What ~~the hell~~ are you getting at?

KITTY

Don't be American, ducky. It's *so* crude. Now 'arken to me. That 'andsome, wealthy lance-corporal is yours for the asking.

MYRA

How do you know?

KITTY

I know because I worked 'im up to the proper state with my own 'ands. 'E's 'ooked, 'e is.

MYRA

You're a good friend, Kitty . . . but you've been wasting your time.

KITTY

Oh, 'ave I! You wait 'til you've 'ad a little talk with 'im and see what I've done for you.

MYRA

What've you done? What've you said?

KITTY

First I found out 'ow much 'e knew, which was nothing. From there, I went on to inform 'im of the facts. I told 'im you was a daughter of the aristocracy, travelling incog.

MYRA

Did he laugh?

KITTY

No, 'e didn't laugh. Not 'im. 'E only sat there, polishing 'is buttons, and swallowing everything. 'E took it so 'ard I give you my word I thought 'e'd bust into tears. So I told him 'ow the war 'ad ruined you—only in a financial way, of course—and of 'ow brave and 'eroic you've been in the face of adversity, and of 'ow you couldn't 'old out much longer.

MYRA

Against what?

KITTY

Against a life of shame. I said—"The only thing on God's earth that'll save 'er," I said, "is a 'usband."

MYRA

A husband?

KITTY

Yes—I appealed to everything that was manly in 'im, and 'e wasn't slow to respond. Oh—you may think 'e looks stupid, but 'e catches on if you put it right. 'E knew what I meant—an' 'e's ready to step up and do 'is duty for King and country. I give you my word, and strike me

dead if I exaggerate, that lad'll marry you to-day
—and what's more, I'm prepared to be your
bridesmaid and 'elp you blush.

MYRA

Did he tell you he was going to marry me?

KITTY

Not quite. 'E was coming to that, though,
when you burst in and interrupted 'im. But I 'ad
'im at the point, and it won't take you more'n ten
minutes to lead 'im past it and finish the job.
'E's yours, I tell you.

MYRA

What if I don't want him?

KITTY

And what if you don't? Of what odds is that?
All you 'ave to do is go through with the cere-
mony and then sleep with 'im a few times 'til 'is
leave is over—and after that, you sit back and
collect 'is assignments and separation allowance
and live in luxury. And there's your insurance if
'e gets knocked off in action . . .

MYRA (*savagely*)

Oh, God—I don't *want* his insurance! And I
don't want to steal any of his pay away from him,
either!

KITTY

Who says it's stealing? Marriage is legal,
ain't it? Why, it's 'oly! Look at what others do.
Look at Agnes 'Enning. She 'as four 'usbands
in the army—two Australians, one Yorkshire-
man and 'er own 'usband what she married before
the war. She's collecting separation allowances
from all of them. And what's more, she's making
'em all 'appy. Every one of them finds the war
easier to bear because 'e's got a little wife waitin'
for 'im 'ere in Blighty. Of course, with Agnes
there is the risk that two of her 'usbands might
'appen to get leave at the same time. But that
wouldn't bother you, with only one on your 'ands.
The only responsibility you'll 'ave is giving 'im
what he wants when 'e's in London, and you
oughtn't to 'ave much trouble doing that. 'Eaven
knows, you've 'ad enough experience.

MYRA

Yes—and what's going to happen to him, and
to me, after the war?

KITTY (*with disgust*)

Oh, you *are* an optimist. After the war! And
when will that be? To-morrow? No! Next year?
No! A 'undred years from now? I doubt it. And
where will you be, or me, or this Canadian, after
the war? The lot of us will be singing bloody
'armony in a place where there ain't no street

walkers or soldiers neither. After the war! You
might as well say you won't put your money in
a bank because there won't be any banks when
the world 'as come to an end. (*There is a distinct pause.*) Well—ain't you got a word to say
to me?

MYRA

No . . . I couldn't get mad at you, Kitty.

KITTY

I should 'ope not, after all I've done to put you
in the way of a good thing.

MYRA

It isn't a good thing, Kitty. It's a stinking
thing.

KITTY

What's stinking about it, I'd like to know? 'E
loves you, don't 'e? Of course 'e does. Look at
the flowers he brought.

MYRA

Flowers?

KITTY (*indicating them*)

Yes, flowers! Bought them in Covent Garden,
'e did. . . . Now tell me 'e don't love you.

MYRA (*looking at the flowers*)

He don't even know me. And he never will
know me, or about me, if I have to go down and

jump off Waterloo Bridge, into the river, to keep him from finding out.

KITTY

Oh—the river! That's the remedy for all things, ain't it? You little fool! You think everything will be settled if 'e goes back into the war and you into the Thames. Never in all my life did I ever 'ear of such stupidity.

MYRA

Maybe you never saw a man before, decent, like he is.

KITTY

Maybe I didn't! And I don't expect to see one soon again—nor will you. Which is just precisely what I've been talking about. You won't 'ave another chance to match this one.

MYRA

I ain't asking for another like him.

KITTY

Then what are you asking for? The Prince of Wales, or the whole brigade of Guards, or what?

MYRA

I'm only asking to get rid of him—to get him out of London—to never see him again . . .

KITTY (*dumfounded*)

You've bloody well gone queer in the 'ead,

that's what you've done. You ought to be sent to
the . . .

(*There is a knock at the door.*)

MYRA

Come in.

(ROY *comes in. He is obviously crestfallen.*)

ROY

Say—I got some bad news.

KITTY

No!

MYRA

What is it, Roy?

ROY

When I was coming out of the Post Office an
M. P. nabbed me.

KITTY

What? Are you A. W. L.?

ROY

No—I'm all right on that—but he asked to
see my pass and then he told me that all leave is
cancelled.

MYRA

What does that mean?

ROY

I've got to get back on duty.

MYRA

But—can they do that?

ROY

You bet they can.

MYRA

When they've promised you fourteen days?

ROY

· Aw—they don't promise a thing. They just tell you.

KITTY

But what's the reason for it?

ROY

I guess there's plenty of reason. There's been a terrible "do" up in the salient.

KITTY

But we won it, didn't we? We took that ridge, whatever its name is.

ROY

Yes, and *we* lost about half the Canadian corps doing it. Anyway, I've got to report to the M. O. at Bramshott for physical examination to see if I'm fit to go back up the line. In a couple of days I'll be heaving on the channel.

MYRA

When do you have to go, Roy?

Roy

I've got to be there at 8 A. M. to-morrow morning. That means I'll have to take the last train out to-night.

Kitty

It's a rotten shame. Can't they give a man breathing space after 'e gets out of hospital before they send 'im back to expose 'isself again?

Roy

Oh, they've got to hold the line somehow. . . . But it's a tough break, all right. I was just beginning to look forward to this leave.

Kitty

Well—I shouldn't be surprised if you didn't want me 'anging around, when your time's so short . . . I'll be seeing you soon, Myra—unless you're planning to leave London?

Myra

No—I won't be leaving London.

Kitty

Don't! (*She extends her hand to* Roy.) Good-by, Canada.

Roy (*shaking her hand*)

Good-by—and thanks, for a lot of things.

Kitty

Thank me for nothing, I'm afraid. 'Owever—

over the top with the best of luck and don't let anything 'appen to stop our favorite war.

Roy

I'll see to that. (KITTY *goes out.*) She's all right.

Myra

I'm awful sorry, Roy.

Roy

Oh, it's just part of the army. (*He is putting his cleaning kit back in his haversack.*)

Myra

That Medical Officer isn't going to make you go back to the trenches. He'll see that you've got to have a lot of easy training before you're fit again.

Roy

He'll just take one look at me and write me down A. 1. That's what he's there for. You see, Myra—they've just simply got to have men. The way they've been dropping 'em lately between Cambrai and Passchendaele they'll take anybody that can stagger up the communication trench.

Myra

I want to thank you for those flowers, Roy.

Roy

Oh—those . . .

MYRA

It was very sweet of you. . . . If you leave me your address, I'll send you those socks. What size shoe do you wear?

ROY

I'll leave you my address all right. But I'm going to leave you something else, too.

MYRA (*alarmed*)

I don't want anything else.

ROY

Listen, Myra—this is a sort of a delicate subject—but, how are you fixed for money?

MYRA

I'm absolutely all right. I don't need a thing.

ROY

I've heard different.

MYRA

I know—Kitty's probably been telling you that I'm hard up.

ROY

As a matter of fact, she has. But she didn't need . . .

MYRA

She doesn't know a thing about it. She doesn't know about—about my private income.

ROY

You've got a private income?

MYRA

Certainly I have. I've never said much about it, but . . .

ROY

Where does it come from?

MYRA

I get it from my folks, back home.

ROY

They're rich, are they?

MYRA (*with assurance*)

Oh, sure—*they* never have to worry about money.

ROY

How much do they send you? A couple of postage stamps now and then so's you can write home?

MYRA

Don't you insult my family! I guess they can take care of their daughter, wherever she is.

ROY

I didn't mean to be nasty. But if it's real money they send you, why do you have to live in a place like this—why do you wear clothes that

anybody can see are old—why did you tell me
last night you'd never had enough to buy a ticket
home? And why do you have to go out now and
get a job?

MYRA

Well—what they send me isn't a million dollars a year.

ROY

I guess I know how much it is, Myra. It isn't
a damned cent. You've been lying to me just to
make me . . .

MYRA (*vehemently*)

What business is it of yours, I'd like to know.
Who gave you a right to question me about my
personal affairs?

ROY

I gave myself the right.

MYRA

And how'd you manage to do that?

ROY

By loving you, that's how.

MYRA (*in a twisted voice*)

Oh—Roy—you can't do that.

ROY

Oh, I can't, can't I? Well, just watch me . . .

MYRA (*fiercely*)

No, Roy—I tell you, you can't—it isn't possible!

ROY

What's the matter, Myra? Why do you say that? Why can't I love you?

MYRA

Because it's wrong—it's wrong!

ROY

It is not. I know what's right and what isn't. How could there be anything wrong about love?

MYRA

There can be everything wrong about it.

ROY

Not the kind of love I have for you. That's—that's good love.

MYRA

I know it, Roy.

ROY

Then if you know it, why are you standing there telling me it's wrong?

MYRA

Because it just doesn't fit—you loving me . . .

ROY

Oh, Lord. I see what you're driving at. You're

still thinking about me being a Y. M. C. A. boy.
You think I oughtn't to fall in love with anybody
but a choir singer. Can't you get that fool idea
out of your head? I don't care if you were in a
thousand shows, or the circus. I love you.

MYRA

No, you don't, Roy.

ROY

Who says I don't?

MYRA

I say it—and I know it. Because you're just
kidding yourself about this love. Don't you see
what's led up to it? You're not in any state to
know what you're talking about.

ROY

You mean you think I'm crazy?

MYRA

No—you're lonesome, Roy. That's the trouble
with you. You've been away from home for three
years—in a strange army—in hospitals—in a
war. You go on leave and get a few days to yourself, and then you meet a girl that sounds like
home. And all of a sudden you find out that
you've been aching for a woman, any woman. I
don't mean by that anything—anything out of
the way. It's just companionship. Your heart

is sick because it's been empty so long. And when you find somebody you can talk to, your heart fills all up, and you mistake it for love.

Roy

It's filled up, all right. It's filled up with you.

Myra

It isn't me, Roy. It's your loneliness. That's what makes you see things all wrong.

Roy (*vehemently*)

Oh, does it! Well, did you ever hear of any man falling in love with any girl for any other reason?

Myra

Loneliness doesn't last, Roy—neither does that kind of love.

Roy

I guess I can take my chances on that.

Myra

Wait 'til you get back to your own people, and you're happy and peaceful—and then see how much you think about me.

Roy

I'm not going to wait that long. I may never see any of 'em again. And if I didn't have you with me, I wouldn't want to see them. I'd rather get a napoo in France and have it over with.

MYRA

You'd be better off—that way—than married to me.

ROY (*hesitantly*)

Are you maybe thinking a little about your own family?

MYRA

What do you mean?

ROY

I mean—are you thinking that you wouldn't want to get married to a kind of a hick, that you'd be ashamed to introduce to your own folks?

MYRA

Yes, Roy—that's one of the things. I'd be ashamed to introduce you to my parents if they were still living, which they aren't, thank God! And do you want to know why I'd be ashamed? Because my father and mother were a couple of drunken bums. They lived in East St. Louis, that exclusive suburb. That's where I come from. I ran away and went on the stage because I was scared to stay in my own home. I was scared one or the other of them might kill me while they were liquored. That's how much aristocracy I am.

Roy (*after a brief pause*)

And you talk about *me* being lonely. Me—
with everything I've got . . .

MYRA

That's it, Roy. You've got enough in your own
life . . .

ROY

And what have you got? What have you
to . . .

MYRA

I can take care of myself! (*She walks away
from him. He turns and looks at her, utterly
unable to comprehend her stubbornness.*)

ROY

Is there anybody at all—I mean any man—
that you're in love with . . .?

MYRA

No, there isn't.

ROY

Or even some one that you used to love—that
you were promised to—like some soldier that was
killed in the war?

MYRA

I never loved any one.

ROY

Then I'm not going to stand here and argue

any more. (*He goes to her, takes hold of her arms, and looks into her face.*) Let me look at you. (*She looks down.*) Don't hold your head like that. Look at me. (*She raises her eyes. After a moment she goes into his arms, clutching him.*)

MYRA (*half strangled*)

Roy!

ROY (*incoherently*)

Don't say anything more, sweetheart. . . . I know how it is. You just don't want to let me get into this, because you think I might regret it some day or other. . . . That's all right. . . . I'm not going to regret this—ever—ever. . . . I guess I know who I was made for, who I've been waiting for all this time. . . . I guess I know who it is I love and worship. (*He releases her and steps back. She has been rigid in his arms and remains so.*) Now—there's a lot we've got to do —and we've got to do it fast.

MYRA (*dully*)

What?

ROY

Well—I guess we've got to see about getting a license. Do you know anything about the laws over here? (MYRA *shakes her head.*) Well—we'll soon find out. Do you know any ministers?

MYRA

No, I don't know any ministers.

Roy

What's your religious faith?

Myra

I'm a Roman Catholic.

Roy

Well—that will be all right. We'll find a priest. And then there'll be a lot of red tape to go through with about my pay book. But that'll be easy. I know a man in the pay office—Captain Faulkner, he used to be with my battalion but he got crippled on the Somme. He's a friend of mine. But we'll have to make it pretty fast, so we can get everything done before I leave to-night. You'd better get your hat on right away.

Myra

Do I have to go with you?

Roy

Sure you have to go. You're a party to this.

Myra

I mean—couldn't you go first and make the arrangements, and then I could meet you some place?

Roy

No—because the first thing is to get a license, and you'll certainly have to sign that.

MYRA

Yes—certainly.

ROY

So, come on—Myra. Snap it up and we'll get started.

MYRA

Roy!

ROY

What is it, Myra?

MYRA

I want to change my dress. Would you mind . . .?

ROY

Waiting outside? Why, sure. (*He goes to the door.*) But please—please make it fast.

MYRA

Yes, Roy.

(*He goes out. She instantly jams on her hat and seizes her suitcase. She tiptoes to the window and looks out over the roof toward* KITTY's. *Then she comes back to the table in the centre, opens a drawer, fishes around in it until she finds a writing tablet and a pencil, and then scrawls a brief note. She tears the page from the tablet, folds it, and stands it up on the table like a tent. She goes over to the wash-stand and takes two or three of the flowers from the pitcher. Then she goes back to the window, picks up her suitcase, gives one look toward the door, and goes out the window and disappears.)*

(For a few moments there is absolute silence. Then the sound of MRS. HOBLEY's *strident voice is heard from the hall outside, mingling with* ROY's. *She seems to be saying, violently, "I tell you, 'e saw 'er," "Down over the roof," "Let me in there"; he is saying, "You're mistaken." "She's in there now," "Tell him he's crazy." There is a peremptory banging on the door.* ROY *calls* "MYRA—*tell her you're there."* MRS. HOBLEY *says, "I'll see for myself."* MRS. HOBLEY *thrusts open the door and strides in, followed hesitantly by* ROY.)

ROY *(in the door)*

Is it all right to come in?

*(*MRS. HOBLEY *looks around the room, then goes to the window and looks out. She then turns to* ROY.)

MRS. HOBLEY

Well—where is she?

ROY

She must be here. Myra! *(He goes to the window.)*

MRS. HOBLEY

Why waste your breath? Can't you see **for** yourself?

Roy (*going to the right*)

Myra! Is there any other door here?

MRS. HOBLEY

There's no other door, bar that one.

ROY

She *couldn't* have gone out of that. I was right there. (*He goes to the curtained wardrobe at the left.*) Myra!

MRS. HOBLEY

She's gone out there, I tell you. Over the roof and through the next 'ouse to the street. My nephew saw her with his own eyes.

ROY (*returning to the window*)

We'd better go next door and see if . . .

MRS. HOBLEY

It's no use doing that. She's in the tube by now, 'eaded 'eaven knows where. She's 'opped it, that's what she's done.

ROY

There must have been some special reason for her doing that. She couldn't have . . .

MRS. HOBLEY

Oh, wasn't there just! She 'ad to get out without 'aving to face me!

Roy (*coming down*)

Why?

MRS. HOBLEY

You know well enough, you 'ypocrite.

Roy (*bewildered*)

Me?

MRS. HOBLEY

Yes, you! It's a conspiracy to fraud me . . .

Roy

Did she owe you money?

MRS. HOBLEY

Did she owe me money! You think I don't know that she posted you deliberately out there to keep me off, while she made good 'er escape. And now you think you can just march out and meet 'er at the agreed spot. Well, I won't 'ave it. I'll 'ave the police on both of you, I will. I won't be cheated and robbed by you and that little 'arlot.

Roy

What did you call her?

MRS. HOBLEY

I called 'er what she is—a filthy little 'arlot.

Roy (*trembling*)

Aren't you kind of careless with what you say?

Mrs. Hobley

No—I'm choosing my words carefully—more carefully than I choose my lodgers. (*She is on the verge of tears.*) I'd like to keep my 'ouse respectable. God knows, it ain't like me to encourage vice. But 'ow am I going to live in these wicked times, and my poor 'usband suffering torture and slow death in a 'Un prison, and food more precious than jewels . . .

Roy

Never mind the grousing. You said something that . . .

Mrs. Hobley

You think I'm conducting a fast 'ouse 'ere because I let rooms to the likes of 'er, because I make no complaint when she 'as men in 'er rooms, night after night, because I accept from 'er the money she takes from them. You think you can insult me and scorn me and cheat me of my just due. Well, you can't! You or your tart, either. You may not know it, Canadian, but there's law in this land . . .

Roy

How much does she owe you? (*He is taking out his pay book, in which are folded some bank-notes.*)

Mrs. Hobley

You mean—you'll pay me?

Roy

That's what I mean.

Mrs. Hobley

That's kind of you, sir. You're a gentleman, you are—which is more'n I can say for most of the soldiers she's 'ad in 'ere.

Roy

I asked you how much she owes you.

Mrs. Hobley

Well—there's two pound eighteen owing from April, and then there's a week's advance on the room now . . .

Roy

What's the rent here?

Mrs. Hobley

On this room?

Roy

Yes.

Mrs. Hobley

Thirty shillings a week.

Roy (*slowly*)

Thirty and forty is seventy, and eighteen, did you say?

Mrs. Hobley

Eighteen—quite correct, sir.

Roy

That's eighty-eight shillings—four pounds eight. (*He takes a five-pound note and a one-pound note and hands them to her.*) There's six pounds. That'll pay what she owes you, and two weeks in advance on this room, with a little to spare. You can credit that.

Mrs. Hobley

Oh—thank you, sir—and God bless you for a . . .

Roy

Kindly give me a receipt for that.

Mrs. Hobley

Gladly, sir. (*She goes to the table, and writes the receipt on the tablet. He starts to fasten the strap on his haversack.*)

Roy

Just make it out that you received it from her.

Mrs. Hobley

Yes, sir. . . . There you are, sir. (*She hands him the receipt.*)

Roy

Thanks. (*He starts toward the door, then turns.*) Where would I be likely to find her?

MRS. HOBLEY

Probably along the Strand, Leicester Square, Piccadilly—those are the regular places for prostitutes like 'er. And then of course there's Waterloo Bridge. Many of 'em 'aunt that to catch the soldiers coming in on leave. (*Again he starts for the door. She notices the note on the table, picks it up and reads it.*) Just a moment, sir.

ROY

What?

MRS. HOBLEY

She seems to 'ave left a note.

ROY

For me?

MRS. HOBLEY

It don't say who it's for. It just says, "I can't do it. Good-by." That's all. (ROY *takes the note from her and looks at it.*) It's none of my affair, sir, what you do or what you don't do. But I know 'er, and I know 'er kind, to my cost. And if you take my advice, sir, when you meet 'er you'll take that receipt and you'll throw it in 'er painted face, and then 'ave no more to do with 'er. Because traffic with 'arlots leads only to sin, and sin leads to suffering. And a soldier like you, sir, 'as enough of suffering in this awful war without 'aving to be contaminated and robbed by loose women of the streets.

Roy (*walking toward the door*)

Oh, shut your God-damned face. (*He goes out.*)

CURTAIN

(*During the brief intermission the sounds of the artillery, sirens and bugles again are heard, indicative of another air-raid.*)

ACT II
SCENE II

ACT II

SCENE II

The bay on Waterloo Bridge. It is late at night. MYRA *is sitting on the bench, huddled into a corner.*

The special constable rides across, shouting as before, "Take cover! Take cover!"

An elderly LABORER *and his* WIFE *run in from the right. He, seeing* MYRA, *stops.*

LABORER

'Old 'ard—what's this?

WIFE

Come along, Charlie. *'Urry!*

LABORER

Wait a mo'. (*He speaks to* MYRA.) What's wrong, Miss?

MYRA

Nothing's wrong. I'm all right.

LABORER

Then come on. You can't stay 'ere.

WIFE

You come on yourself!

159

MYRA

Don't mind me. I want to stay here.

LABORER

But Jerry's up. It's a air-raid.

MYRA

I know . . .

WIFE

Leave 'er alone, Charlie. Do you want to get us both killed?

LABORER

Are you sick, Miss?

MYRA

No—honestly. I'm perfectly all right.

WIFE

It's 'er own concern, Charlie. Come *on!* I'm frightened . . .

MYRA

Go ahead, please.

LABORER

All right, Miss. I expect you know what . . .

WIFE

For God's sake, run. . . .

(*There is a loud explosion near at hand. A bomb has landed on the embankment. The* LABORER *and his wife run out at the left.*)

(Roy *comes in from the right. He sees* Myra
*before she sees him, and is close to her before she
looks up. When she sees him staring at her, she
utters a little cry.*)

Roy (*in a strained voice*)

I've been looking for you. I'd about given up
hope of finding you.

Myra

You oughtn't to have tried to find me.

Roy

I've been walking backward and forward on this
bridge, and up and down the Strand and Leicester Square and Piccadilly for hours. She told me
that was your regular beat.

Myra

Who—told you that?

Roy

Mrs. Hobley.

Myra

Oh—you talked to her?

Roy

Yes.

Myra

I was afraid you would . . .

Roy

I got your note.

Myra

Well—there wasn't anything else for me to say.

Roy (*harshly*)

Wasn't there?

Myra

Nothing more that—that I wanted to say, to you.

Roy

I guess not. But I wanted to find you. I had to give you something. (*He takes out his pay book and extracts from it the receipt* Mrs. Hobley *had given him.*) Here's a receipt from Mrs. Hobley. It covers two weeks' advance rent on your room. (*He hands it to her.*)

Myra

I didn't want you . . .

Roy

And here's something else you'd better take. I went to the pay corps office and made an arrangement for an assignment—they turn over so much a month out of my pay to you. You'll have to go in there to-morrow with this card and sign a paper they'll give you. Ask for Capt. Faulkner when you get there. He knows all about it. He'll take care of you, all right. It isn't much money, but

still . . . I'd just like to know you were getting
it. . . . Be sure to ask for Capt. Faulkner. . . .
I guess that's all. (*He looks at his wrist watch.*)
I've got to get an eleven fourteen train at Waterloo.

(*She is holding the receipt and the card in her
hand. Suddenly she bursts into convulsive, hyster-
ical sobs. For a while, he stands watching her,
dumbly.*)

Roy

Don't cry, Myra—don't cry like that . . .

Myra (*wildly*)

Go away—go away!

Roy

I can't stand to hear you cry like that!

Myra

Go away to your train.

Roy (*coming closer to her*)

I can't stand it, I tell you—when I've been
fighting all day to keep hold of myself, and not
blurt out all the things I've wanted to say. I
knew the only way to make it easy for you was
just to show you what I think, and then go, without making any fuss . . . and then you sit there,
crying!

MYRA

You've got to stop thinking about me.

ROY

Ask me to stop breathing! It'd be easier . . .

MYRA

You've got to do it—that's all.

ROY

I don't have to do it. I don't have to do anything that's impossible, do I?

(*He sits down on the bench beside her and makes a fierce but awkward attempt to take her in his arms. She twists herself away from him.*)

MYRA

It's late, Roy. You've got to go to your train.

ROY

Listen, Myra—supposing I don't go to that train?

MYRA (*standing up*)

Oh—but you've got to. It's the last . . .

ROY

Who says I've got to?

MYRA

They told you to be there, to report . . .

Roy

They! Who's they! A lot of damned officers that want men. They want men so they can take another ridge—and lose it again. Well, I've done enough of that. I've got other things to do. They can all go to hell! I'm going to say here, with you . . .

Myra

You can't do that, Roy. They gave you orders . . .

Roy

All I have to do is miss that train—and that's all I'm going to do. To-morrow they're going to be expecting me at the camp and I won't be there.

Myra

They'll send the M. P.'s to arrest you.

Roy

What difference is it to me what they do? I'm *finished* with them. They don't own me any more. They can have their number back, because I won't be using it from now on. I love you, sweetheart. Do you hear that? Do you understand what that means? My life is yours, not theirs.

Myra

You can't get out that way, Roy.

Roy

Oh, can't I! For three years I've done everything they told me. I've sloped arms when they told me and saluted when they told me; I've stood up straight when they told me and ducked when they told me. For three years I've played their game. Now, by God, I'm going to play my own.

MYRA

It's no use talking big like that, Roy. It isn't your game.

ROY

I'm the best judge as to that. I guess I know when I'm through with their war. It's time they found out that human beings can't go on obeying them forever. . . . I've found you. That makes everything different.

MYRA

Not you, Roy. Why, you're a model soldier, and nothing will ever make you different. You belong with them, doing what they tell you to. You can't change yourself, Roy. And you can't let yourself down.

ROY (*harshly*)

Listen, Myra, there's something I want you to tell me. . . . Do you love me?

MYRA

That hasn't got anything to do with your going . . .

Roy

It's got everything to do with it. Why did you come here, to this bridge, and wait here—when you knew I'd have to go this way . . .

Myra

I was a fool to do it. I knew I was a fool. But I had to, Roy. I thought I could hide here, and then you'd go by and never notice me. I had to see you just once more.

Roy

Then you do feel—something about me—that you didn't feel about those others . . .

Myra

I love you, Roy. I love you . . . I love everything about you—everything you are. I didn't know I coud love anybody, until—until you said we ought to get married. But I know it now, Roy —and I always will know it, and I'll always be thankful for it. . . .

Roy

Then that's the answer, isn't it? We love each other—we belong to each other.

Myra

No, Roy! I don't belong in the same lifetime with you. I'm a whore!

(*He has relaxed his hold on her, but now he seizes her again in his arms and presses her face against him as though to silence her.*)

Roy (*passionately*)

You're not! You're good! I know it. I'll swear it before God!

MYRA

All right, then, prove it to Him. Prove to Him that I didn't break your life in two. Let Him see that I sent you back to the line, to fight the war. Make Him know that . . .

Roy

Yes—fight the war! What's the war, anyway? It's that guy up there in his aeroplane. What do I care about him and his bombs? (*He goes to the wall and leans over it as though beyond it were a vast crowd listening to him.*) What do I care who he is, or what he does, or what happens to him? That war's over for me. What I've got to fight is the whole dirty world. That's the enemy that's against you and me. That's what makes the rotten mess we've got to live in. . . . Look at them— shooting their guns up into the air, firing their little shells at something they can't even see. Why don't they turn their guns down into the streets, and shoot at what's there? Why don't they be merciful and kill the people that want to be killed? . . . Oh God—if they'd ever stopped to figure things out the way I've had to do, the whole lot of them would be committing suicide instead of shooting into the air.

MYRA

Roy—you mustn't get excited like that.

ROY

I know—it's a waste of breath—they can't
hear me.

(*Through the latter part of* ROY's *long speech
the faint sounds of an airplane have been heard
growing louder and louder. There is now a burst
of machine-gun fire and the crash of a bomb, driving them into each other's arms. The noise sub-
sides as the plane goes elsewhere.*)

MYRA

You want to do something for me, don't you,
Roy?

ROY

Yes. (*His voice is now dead. He has had his
say.*)

MYRA

You want to make me happy, don't you?

ROY

Yes.

MYRA

You want me to know that you know I'm not—
what I'm . . .

ROY

Yes!

MYRA

Then get to that train.

Roy

And go back to the line and get knocked off and never see you again?

Myra

That isn't the point.

Roy

I wish I knew what *is* the point.

Myra

You will. . . . . What's your address in France, Roy?

Roy

It's on that card I gave you——

Myra

I'll send you those socks.

Roy

And what are you going to do?

Myra

I'll be all right.

Roy

It's easy to say that.

Myra

It's easier to mean it, now.

Roy

If I get that train, will you go back to your room?

MYRA

Yes.

ROY

And sign that paper at the pay office to-morrow?

MYRA (*with reluctance*)

Yes, Roy. . . . Now please go.

ROY

Oh—I forgot to tell you—there'll be some insurance, quite a lot of it, if I get . . .

MYRA

Don't say that, Roy! You're going to come through fine. You're going to live, and get back to your folks and forget about everything bad that's happened . . .

ROY

Forget! God Almighty! What's going to make me forget? What's going to make me get out of my mind what's been burned in there?

(*The* MILITARY POLICEMAN *comes in from the right, briskly. He is wearing a tin hat. He sees* ROY *and stops.*)

MILITARY POLICEMAN

What are you doing 'ere, soldier?

ROY

Leave me alone.

MILITARY POLICEMAN

Let's 'ave a look at your pass.

MYRA

It's all right, policeman. He's going to that 11:14 train.

MILITARY POLICEMAN

Then I'll just go along with you and 'elp you find the station.

ROY

I know where it is. . . . (*He stares at* MYRA.) . . . Good-by.

(*The* MILITARY POLICEMAN *stands at the left, waiting.*)

MYRA

Good-by, Roy. . . . You might write me a letter, once in a while?

ROY

I will.

MYRA

And I hope the socks will fit.

ROY

They'll fit.

MILITARY POLICEMAN

Come on, soldier.

ROY

I'll try to get back, some time.

MYRA

That's right, Roy. Good-by.

(*He kisses her.*)

ROY

Good-by, darling.

(*He goes out at the left.*)

(*The sound of the German airplane is again heard, circling back from Westminster. A machine-gun on the embankment is firing at it. The* MILITARY POLICEMAN *looks up.*)

MILITARY POLICEMAN

Better be getting off this bridge, Miss. It's dangerous.

(MYRA *turns and starts to go toward the right, slowly. The* MILITARY POLICEMAN *turns and goes out at the left, quickly. The motor of the Gotha bomber is droning directly overhead.* MYRA *looks upward, and pauses. Then she opens her handbag and takes from it the wilted package of Camels. She takes one and lights it, very deliberately.*)

MYRA (*looking upward*)

Here I am, Heinie . . . I'm right down here. . . .

(*She holds up the lighted match.*)

CURTAIN